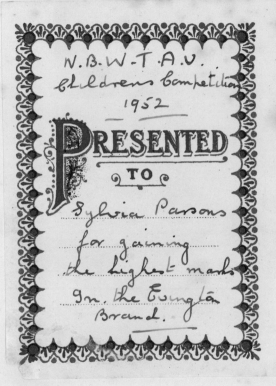

N.B.W.T.A.V.
Childrens Competition
1952

PRESENTED

TO

Sylvia Parsons
for gaining
the highest marks
In the Evington
Brand.

A Rebel Schoolgirl

BLACKIE & SON LIMITED
66 Chandos Place, LONDON
17 Stanhope Street, GLASGOW

BLACKIE & SON (INDIA) LIMITED
103/5 Fort Street, BOMBAY

BLACKIE & SON (CANADA) LIMITED
TORONTO

" I CAN'T STAY HERE!"

Page 171   *Frontispiece*

F 353

"I CAN'T STAY HERE!"

Page 171

Frontispiece

A Rebel Schoolgirl

BY

FRANCES CARPENTER

With frontispiece by F. G. Moorsom

BLACKIE & SON LIMITED
LONDON AND GLASGOW

Printed in Great Britain by Blackie & Son, Ltd., Glasgow

Contents

A REBEL SCHOOLGIRL

CHAPTER I

Betty Raises her Standard

Feet pattered on worn paving-stones, dark heads and fair heads bobbed excitedly, as about twenty senior girls of Windmill School made their way across the courtyard. There was a buzz of voices, though none of them was raised very high.

" It's an indignation meeting!"

" Betty Lyndon's going to take the chair. It's a protest against the new Head!"

" Betty's going to lead a rebellion, I believe!"

" The dogs of war are let loose," quoted a short stumpy girl named Mary Towle, whose arm was linked as usual in that of her chum, Sonia Starforth.

" I'm thrilled!" declared Sonia, tossing her fair plaits. " I suppose I feel it more than some of the others, Mary, because of my ancestors. They've so often fought for the right against the wrong, you know. There was Sir Steven Starforth, the Cavalier, who——"

" I say, Sonia, have any of your ancestors ever lisped?" drawled Esme Randall, who was walking close behind them.

" Lisped?" echoed Sonia. " Not as far as I know—it's not mentioned in the family records. But why in the world do you want to know?"

" Only because it would have been so very awkward for them," replied Esme. " Their names all seem to have begun with an S, and just fancy your Cavalier ancestor going up to King Charles and saying, ' Pleath, thir, I'm Thir Thteven Thtarforth '."

A burst of laughter broke from the group around them, for teasing Sonia about her ancestors was one of the favourite pastimes at Windmill, in which everyone joined—except loyal Mary.

" Never mind, Sonia," Mary said, her spectacles flashing wisely. " He laughs best who laughs last, you know!"

By this time the girls had reached a round brick structure at the end of the west wing, and separated from it by a short covered passage.

Visitors to the school were always struck by this feature. After they had admired the mellow red brick and pleasant Tudor gables of the main buildings, which were built round three sides of the courtyard, they would turn to the round structure with an air of surprise and inquiry.

Then girls would proudly explain that this was the base of the original windmill which had stood on that spot for centuries, and from which the school had taken its name. Only the base of it was left now, and this had been roofed over and converted into a common-room for the senior girls.

Legends clustered thickly around the old mill. It was said that Mary Towle—that keen student of history—could hold forth for an hour on the subject, beginning with that memorable night when King Charles had taken shelter in the mill, and his loyal followers had drunk his health there by candle-light, while the Roundheads searched for him not many miles away.

No wonder the senior girls of Windmill School were proud of their common-room!

It was certainly a pleasant place, its circular

wall pierced by casement windows, and a wide brick hearth on which a fire was crackling. There was an old oak refectory table in the middle, several cosy chairs dotted about, and lockers ranged round the wall.

Hung in a place of honour was the portrait of Miss Priscilla Jennings—affectionately known as " Prissy "—who had been head mistress of Windmill School for thirty years, until her retirement at the end of the previous term.

With that wise, kindly smile on her face, " Prissy " seemed to gaze down at the girls and the school she had loved so well.

" Here comes Betty!" exclaimed Sonia, peeping through the window.

A moment later Betty Lyndon ran into the room, brushing her wavy brown hair away from her eyes. Although there was no official head girl of the school, Betty was their acknowledged leader, and the best hockey and tennis player the school had ever known.

" Here, let's hike Esme out of the big armchair, and let Betty take it!" exclaimed Hilda Field. " Out you come, Esme—Betty's going to take the chair."

Tall, graceful Esme Randall had the knack of dropping, in an artistic pose, into the most comfortable chair of any room she happened to enter.

" Oh, never mind about the chair!" cried Betty.

With one bound she vaulted on to the table and gazed around at the girls, her wide-set hazel eyes glowing.

" You all know why this meeting has been called," Betty Lyndon began. " I take it we are all loyal to dear old Prissy, the finest head mistress any school ever had!"

A chorus of cheers greeted this beginning, but as they died down, Esme Randall was heard to drawl: " But Prissy isn't here any longer, Betty, old thing. We can't be loyal to a head who isn't a head any more."

" We can be loyal to her memory, can't we?" returned Betty, almost fiercely. " It was Prissy who made Windmill into the school we've all loved, and where we've been so happy, and it's up to us to fight to keep Windmill just as Prissy made it, with all its dear old customs and traditions—all the things which, Prissy used to tell us, made up the spirit of the school. Miss Shephard wants to change everything, if she can. You've all heard her hinting that we're behind the times here, and that lots of

things have got to be altered. I suppose she
thinks Prissy was hopelessly old-fashioned, too.
If she has her way, Windmill won't be Windmill any more!"

The fire of Betty's indignation was beginning
to communicate itself to the other girls, and
there were cries of " Hear, hear!" as she
paused for breath.

" I'm not talking about little changes, that
don't matter one way or the other," went on
Betty. " I'm not worried because the getting-
up bell rings at seven instead of eight " (several
loud groans greeted this reference to the new
head's belief in early rising); "most of us used
to get up at seven, anyway. But Miss Shephard isn't content with little things like that—
she is striking at our old customs and traditions.
Take the Candle-light Suppers, for instance."

At this, Sonia Starforth jumped to her feet.

" I'm with you there, Betty!" she exclaimed.
" As one whose ancestors fought for King
Charles, I think it's really insulting and—er—
unpatriotic, to put a stop to the suppers!"

The Candle-light Suppers, as they were
called, had been an institution at Windmill for
more than twenty years. They had been suggested in the first place by the legend which

told of King Charles taking refuge in the mill,
three hundred years ago, and being toasted in
the dim candle-light by his cavaliers.

So Miss Jennings had started her Candle-
light Suppers for the senior girls, and once a
week they would gather in the windmill common-room half an hour before bedtime, candles
would be lighted and lemonade and sausage
rolls enjoyed, while Prissy chatted about his
tory, always taking the old windmill as her
starting-point.

Before this new autumn term had been many
days old, the seniors had learnt that there were
to be no more Candle-light Suppers.

" I don't know how you feel about it, but I
always think those suppers were some of my
happiest times," continued Betty.   " Then
there's compulsory games. Prissy never believed
in making games compulsory, as you know—
she thought it was better for girls to play only
if they were really keen. But, of course, Miss
Audrey Shephard has had to alter that, too.
But there's something far worse than that. I
only heard a rumour about it to-day, and that's
why I called this meeting."

Betty paused, while all eyes were fixed on
her.

" I believe Miss Shephard means to pull down our windmill common-room altogether," she said.

" *What?* "

Even Esme Randall was roused out of her dignified poise now. An outburst of excited questions buzzed round the table on which Betty was standing.

" Pull down the windmill! "

" But why, Betty? It's the very thing the school was named after! "

" Perhaps she'll change the name—call it St. Audrey's College, or something equally fatuous," drawled Esme.

" Our respected new head was very upset to find we hadn't got a really up-to-date chemistry lab here," explained Betty. " It seems she intends to have one built, and the only possible place—according to her—is here at the end of the west wing, where the windmill stands. So if she has her way, down will come our windmill, and up will go a smelly lab! "

The general indignation was cut short by Sonia, who turned from the window with one finger uplifted.

" Hist! " she warned, in a dramatic whisper.

(F 353)

" Here comes the new girl, Hilary What's-her-name—don't forget that she's the tyrant's niece!"

" We're not likely to forget that," put in Esme. " I shouldn't be surprised if Miss Shephard hasn't planted her here to spy on us, so you had better take care what you say now, Betty."

A sudden hush fell on the girls as Hilary Day entered the common-room.

Hilary was not, at first sight, a very pretty or attractive girl, though her thin face was saved from plainness by a pair of candid grey eyes which usually smiled very pleasantly on the world.

It was common knowledge that Hilary had been with Miss Shephard at her old school, and when her aunt had been appointed head of Windmill, Hilary had moved to the new school with her. She had only arrived the previous day, and she now stood looking at the girls inquiringly, swinging some school books from a strap in her hand.

" I believe I'm to have a locker here," she said. " Can anybody tell me if there's one vacant?"

For a moment no one spoke. Then Betty said shortly.

" You can take any empty locker except the ones right at the end, by the fire. They belong to the prefects."

Hilary eyed Betty pleasantly.

" Oh, then I suppose I'm to have one of those," she replied. " You see, I was a prefect at Miss Shephard's old school, and she tells me she wishes me to continue as a prefect here."

So saying, Hilary strolled towards the privileged lockers, swinging her bundle of books, just as if she had not dropped a kind of bombshell amongst the seniors. A new girl appointed prefect! Such a thing had never been heard of at Windmill School.

" Well, if that isn't the last straw—the absolute jolly limit!" burst out Betty.

Sitting on a locker, Hilary gazed up at the girls, and for the first time she seemed to be aware of the hostile glances that were being directed towards her, for a faint flush crept into her cheeks.

" Is anything wrong?" she asked.

" Everything's wrong!" retorted Betty. " It's always been the custom here for prefects to be girls who have worked their way up through the school and won their spurs, and learnt to know and love the place. Well, it just shows how much Miss Shephard thinks of Windmill, if she can appoint a new girl to be a prefect on her very first day!"

" We must take care what we say at the prefects' meetings, or one of our number will be trotting off to tell Auntie about us," put in Esme, in her most sarcastic tone.

Except that her colour deepened a little, Hilary took no notice of this remark.

" After all, it's Miss Shephard who appoints the prefects," she said steadily. " I didn't have any choice in the matter."

Betty had swung round to face the others, with that characteristic movement of her hand, brushing the wavy brown hair away from her forehead.

" Well, here is our chance, girls!" she cried. " There are five of us prefects here—Mary, Sonia, Esme, Hilda and myself. We've been wondering what we can do to show Miss Shephard how we hate the changes that are spoiling Windmill. Let's go to the head now and resign our prefectships, as a protest against a new girl being foisted on us. Come along! Let's do it this minute!"

As usual, Betty's impetuous leadership won

the day, though if it had not been for her influence, some of the prefects might have hesitated before taking such a defiant step.

As it was, they flocked eagerly towards Betty, and she led the way out of the common-room and across the courtyard in the direction of Miss Shephard's study.

Hilary sat quietly putting her books away in an empty locker. The rest of the seniors took no notice of her.

Although outwardly she looked so calm, Hilary's thoughts were far from pleasant ones.

" Oh, I wish Auntie hadn't insisted on my being a prefect here," she was thinking. " I felt the girls might resent it, and so they do. I want to be friends with them, and yet I've got to be loyal to Auntie, too."

Poor Hilary! There was a troubled look in her candid grey eyes.

She had a very keen sense of duty, and it was this, as much as anything, that had brought her to Windmill. At her old college, where her aunt, Miss Shephard, had been a mistress, Hilary had been popular and happy, and it had cost her a good many pangs to leave before her school life was ended. Miss Shephard had left her quite free to decide, but somehow

Hilary had felt that her aunt might need her at the new school, and that it was her duty to go.

Hilary had a great admiration for her aunt. She felt quite sure that Miss Shephard would make a splendid head mistress, and that the girls would like her, once they got to know her.

Yet, like a wary sailor eyeing the weather, Hilary could see squalls and rough weather ahead.

" Whatever happens, I must be loyal to Auntie," she decided. " It's my duty."

Meanwhile, five rather uncomfortable prefects were standing in Miss Shephard's oak-panelled study.

The new head was a handsome woman of thirty-six, and a greater contrast with gentle silver-haired " Prissy " could not possibly be imagined. Miss Shephard's hair was jet black, her manner was brisk and decisive, and her voice had a deep contralto ring.

" Well, I am glad my prefects have come to see me," she had smiled, on their entrance. " I think it is high time that we got to know one another better, and as it happens I had intended asking you to take tea with me here to-morrow. Won't you sit down, girls—I think there are chairs enough?"

None of the girls moved. Sonia said afterwards that she had very nearly disgraced the name of Starforth by flying from the study there and then. At last, after an awkward silence, Betty blurted out:

" We've come to resign, Miss Shephard."

For a moment the head's black, level brows drew together. She glanced from one to the other of the girls standing before her. Mary Towle, who had an unfortunate habit of blushing at such moments, felt her cheeks turning a deep crimson.

" Dear me, this is very strange," Miss Shephard said. " May I ask what are your reasons for taking such an extraordinary step?"

Again it was Betty who spoke up.

" We—we're out of sympathy with all the changes that are being made here, Miss Shephard," she said. " We are all girls who've been brought up here under Pris—under Miss Jennings, and we've learnt to love Windmill as it has always been up till now. And more especially we resent having a new girl made a prefect almost on her very first day. The prefects here have always been girls who understand the Windmill traditions. Miss Jennings told us that many times."

Rather breathlessly, Betty finished her little speech, very conscious of the keen searching gaze of Miss Shephard's eyes.

" You are Betty Lyndon, are you not?" asked the head. " Am I to take it that you other girls are genuinely resentful of any changes here, or have you just been carried away by Betty's arguments?"

" Of course they are just as much against it as I——" Betty burst out; but Miss Shephard stopped her with a gesture.

" Let the others speak for themselves, Betty," she said, rather coldly. " Esme Randall, do you wish to resign?"

" Yes, Miss Shephard," replied Esme, with something less than her usual drawl.

" And you, Hilda Field?"

It was typical of Miss Shephard that, although she had only been at Windmill for such a short while, she already knew the prefects and most of the seniors by name, and rarely made a mistake in addressing them.

" Yes, Miss Shephard," said Hilda solemnly.

" And Mary?"

" Yes, Miss Shephard."

" And you, Sonia?"

" Yes, Miss Shephard. You see, my family——"

" That will do, Sonia," interrupted the head. " I won't disguise the fact that I am grieved and disappointed that you five prefects should have seen fit to take such a step. I was hoping to have your loyal help during my first term at Windmill School. Of course, I should be well within my rights if I refused to accept your resignations, but I have no wish to force any girl to act as a prefect if she does not wish to. A prefect should regard her duties as a labour of love and loyalty to her school, should she not? So for the time being, it seems, we shall have only one prefect at Windmill. Very well!"

The girls felt they were dismissed, and were turning away when Miss Shephard rose from her desk. How tall and imposing she looked, with those coils of jet-black hair!

" If any of you wish to change your minds within the next week or two, you will be free to do so," she said. " Try to remember that change is not always a bad thing. Changes must come, and wise folk accept them, and work to make the future better than the past. You may go, girls."

Safely out in the corridor, the ex-prefects heaved sighs of relief.

" Thank goodness that's over," breathed

Mary. " My word, hasn't she got a piercing eye! ' It glows like plated Mars!' "

" For pity's sake, don't give us any more of your drivelling quotations, Owl," exclaimed Esme irritably. " I believe you make them up—nobody knows where they come from."

" Well, I like that! It's from Antony and——"

" Oh, shut up!"

Betty hardly heard what her friends were saying. She was thinking that, last term, it had been her beloved Prissy who had occupied the study in which Miss Shephard was now installed. To Betty's mind, the new head was an interloper—a stranger.

" I hate her—I hate her!" she murmured fiercely.

CHAPTER II

A Skirmish

" Now, has it sunk into your brains, my kidlets? Can you all remember it? Then don't forget to sing it at the top of your voices as soon as she comes in!"

There was a mischievous gleam in the eyes of eleven-year-old Madge Williams, as she gazed at her fellow-members of the junior play-room.

" I can't think how you make up such wonderful poetry, Madge," said Lorna Wood admiringly. " I'm sure I never could, if I tried from now till next Christmas."

" Well, you see, I'm the only one with brains in our family," replied Madge airily. " That's why I can do these things."

A howl of protest came from Madge's twin sister, Maureen. The two of them were known as the Terrible Twins, and well deserved the title!

" You awful cheat, Madge! You know very

well I helped you make it up. I did more than half of it!"

" Oh, you didn't, you terrible twister!"

" I did, you little conceited pig! And I've got more brains than you because I was born three hours earlier, and the oldest one of a pair of twins always has most sense!"

Although they were inseparable chums, the twins were fond of a good squabble, and their arguments and quarrels made the junior playroom a very lively place.

Anyone who knew the juniors at Windmill might have noted that they seemed specially excitable at present. The truth was, they felt they were living in stirring times, and they had thrilled at the news that Betty Lyndon and the other prefects had resigned because they did not like the changes at Windmill, and because they objected to the new prefect, Hilary Day.

The task of keeping order out of school hours was very largely entrusted to the prefects at Windmill. The juniors adored Betty, and most of the other prefects were popular, too.

Now these old well-tried leaders had gone, and in their place stood Hilary Day, the new girl.

Already a feeling of mutiny was spreading

amongst the juniors. Madge and Maureen had been heard loudly declaring that, just because she was the head's niece, they were not going to allow Hilary to " boss " them. They meant to stand by Betty Lyndon and the old prefects.

That was the reason why voices were raised a little more than usual, locker lids were banged a little more loudly, and there was a general air of suspense and excitement.

That war-like pair, Madge and Maureen, had already made plans for the reception of Hilary, when she showed herself in the play-room.

However, for the moment the twins were intent on their own quarrel, and seeking a new angle of attack, Madge was peeping sideways towards a girl who sat at one of the small tables, with a cardboard box in front of her.

This was Isabel Bayley, rather a solitary girl, noted for the number of quaint pets she managed to keep, more or less secretly, in the school. The cardboard box was the home of William of Orange, Isabel's white mouse.

Wrapped in her own thoughts, Isabel was meditating certain changes in William's diet, when to her dismay the box was suddenly snatched from the table.

Looking up, she saw that the box had been grasped by Madge, whose blue eyes were alight with mischief.

" Here, give it back, Madge!" cried Isabel, jumping up in alarm. " It's bad for William to be jerked about like that. What are you going to do? Give it back!"

But already Madge was advancing across the room, the box held high. She knew that her twin sister had an unreasoning terror of mice.

" I'm going to empty William over you, Maureen, if you don't confess that I was the one who wrote that verse!" she threatened.

With a wild scream, Maureen sprang away, hotly pursued by her twin, while poor Isabel followed them, begging for the return of her pet. A table was knocked over, a pile of books went flying, girls dodged this way and that, shouting with laughter.

In the midst of the pandemonium, the door opened.

" I say, do try to make a little less noise, you youngsters!"

It was Hilary's voice. The new prefect stood in the doorway, her cool grey eyes surveying the noisy scene.

A sudden hush fell on the play-room, and

then the impish Madge raised one hand in the manner of someone conducting a choir.

" Now then, girls!" she whispered. " Let it go. One, two, three!"

> " Hilary, Hilary, Hee,
>   We've only got one pre!
>   When she's about
>   We laugh and shout,
>   For nobody cares for *she*!"

The last ungrammatical pronoun was yelled at the top of their young voices, and the " song " was followed by another outbreak of laughing and shouting and stamping, above which Isabel's voice rose in an anxious wail.

" William's got away! Oh, please be careful, everybody! Shut the door, Hilary—quick!"

A small white form could be seen scuttling towards the open doorway, and Hilary hastily closed it, only just in time. With a squeal of triumph, Isabel swooped on her pet, gathering it up in her hands.

" Come along, let's sing our song again, kidlets!" cried Maureen. " All together, and keep time. Hilary, Hilary, Hee——"

It was not the first time Hilary had faced rebellious juniors, but she had never had to meet quite such a hostile crowd as this. She ignored an impulse to rush at the grinning Maureen, catch her by the shoulders, and give her a good shaking. It was while she stood there, a little paler than usual, wondering how to deal with the situation, that the door opened once again and Betty Lyndon stepped in.

" *Betty*!"

At once the tumult died down, as the youngsters caught sight of their favourite senior. Madge and Maureen, who were chief amongst Betty's admirers, rushed towards her, each seizing an arm.

" Come and sit by the fire, Betty!" called Lorna.

" Oh, I'm not stopping," replied Betty, with a glance at Hilary, who stood forgotten by the door. " I've just looked in to tell you two twins that we're playing you both in the Third Eleven to-morrow, Maureen as outside-left, and Madge as inside-left. Mind you play up, kiddies!"

" Oh, Betty, you bet we will!" vowed Madge. " We've been practising hockey no end during the holidays, haven't we, Madge?"

" Rather!" agreed her twin.

" Do come and tell us a story, Betty!" pleaded Lorna.

" No, I must be off," replied Betty. She looked across at Hilary with a curious glint in her brown eyes. " Sorry to interrupt you, Hilary," she added. " Were you giving them a singing lesson? It sounded like it!"

With a cool nod, she turned on her heel and strolled out of the play-room.

No sooner was Betty in the corridor than the tumult broke out again, if anything louder than before. It was just as if the juniors were telling her that they would keep quiet for *her* sake, but would not do so for Hilary's. A little smile of triumph played about Betty's lips.

But the smile died quickly, as she stood listening to the hubbub. It wasn't the sort of thing that ought to happen at Windmill, somehow; a new prefect being ragged by the juniors, with no one to go to her aid. All the generosity in Betty's nature welled up, urging her to go back and help Hilary to restore order in the play-room.

Then her lips tightened, and she shook her head.

" I'm not a prefect any more, and it's not my business," she thought. " Perhaps this sort of thing will prove to Miss Shephard that the juniors are on our side too, and are loyal to

Prissy and her ways. I'm glad they're ragging Hilary!"

So Betty hurried on her way, not sorry when she was out of hearing of the noise.

Hilary, however, had quickly recovered her cool, unruffled manner, in spite of the rebellious din that was going on around her. Rather to the juniors' surprise, she was moving towards a blackboard that was kept in one corner of the room, for use when one of the mistresses gave a friendly talk on some subject of interest to the younger girls.

Hilary's brows were knitted slightly, as she picked up a piece of chalk, and stood with it poised in her hand. Then she began to write in her clear, bold hand:

> "We juniors are merry and bright,
> But our grammar is not always right.
> Though we're scared of a mouse
> If it runs round the house . . ."

It was not, perhaps, a very wonderful limerick, but it was the best Hilary could manage at the moment. So curious were the juniors, wondering what on earth Hilary was up to, that most of them forgot to continue their part in the din.

" I want to know which of you made up that verse you were singing when I came in?" Hilary asked, gazing from one to another of them.

With one accord, the Terrible Twins stepped forward.

" It was me!" cried Madge.

" No, it wasn't, it was me!" exclaimed Maureen.

" You cheat, Madge!"

" You twister, Maureen!"

Hilary laughed.

" Oh, well, I'll give you both credit for doing it," she replied. " Since you are such clever young poets, I want you to stay in here and find a last line to that limerick, and mind that it scans and rhymes properly. Sit at that desk, both of you!"

There was something in the level glance of Hilary's eyes that made the twins obey, though they were murmuring and muttering under their breath. As they sat down, the supper bell rang.

" Poets don't need supper," smiled the new prefect. " Hurry along, all you other girls. Miss Darkin is taking duty to-night, and I don't want to have to report any of you to her,

though, of course, I'll have to explain why
Madge and Maureen aren't there."

Isabel Bayley was the first to slip away,
clasping the cardboard box, intent on finding
some safe haven for William before she went
in to supper. By ones and twos the others followed, with many glances at the twins sitting
mutinously at the little table in front of the
blackboard.

Hilary strolled to the door.

" I shall lock you in," she said. " And mind
that it rhymes and scans, young poets."

She passed outside, and the twins heard the
key turn in the lock.

" What a beast she is!" exclaimed Maureen,
with a vision of steaming cocoa, biscuits and
fruit floating before her hungry eyes.

" Don't let's write a word," said Madge.
" Let's defy her."

Maureen gazed thoughtfully at the blackboard.

" If we don't do anything she'll think it's
because we can't," she said. " We oughtn't
to let ourselves be stumped by a silly limerick,
Madge. Let's think, now!"

Their brown heads close together, the twins
puzzled over their last line, with many giggles
and squabbles.

In the dining-hall, Miss Darkin, seeing two empty chairs, was asking: " Where are the twins?"

" Oh, I told them they could miss supper, Miss Darkin," Hilary answered. " They are busy writing poetry in the play-room."

Miss Darkin was mistress of the Sixth, and she had been at Windmill before Hilary was born. She had the reputation of being a very strict mistress, but she was also a very understanding one, and there was little that escaped her.

She was well aware of the currents of antagonism and even mutiny that were flowing through the school. She noted, too, that Hilary's cheeks were a little paler and thinner than they had been when first she came to Windmill, and she knew something of the loneliness and strain of Hilary's present position.

Beyond giving the new prefect a slight smile, Miss Darkin made no further comment on the absence of the Terrible Twins.

It was about half an hour later when the twins heard the click of the key, and Hilary strolled coolly into the play-room once more.

" Well, how have you been getting on?"

" Oh, we've done it," replied Madge and Maureen in one breath, pushing a rather grubby piece of paper towards Hilary, who picked it up and read the completed limerick:

> "We juniors are merry and bright,
>   But our grammar is not always right.
>   Though we're scared of a mouse
>   If it runs round the house,
>   A new prefect can't give us a fright!"

" H'm! It's rather cheeky," said Hilary. " Still, it rhymes and scans, more or less, so I suppose it will do."

Giggling, the twins jumped to their feet.

" Can we go up to bed now?" demanded Madge.

" Just wait a minute," Hilary said, turning and walking back towards the door. She stepped outside, and to the amazement of the twins, came back pushing a dinner wagon on which were two cups of hot cocoa, a plate of biscuits and two apples.

" You need some nourishment after all that brain-fag, I'm sure," she said. " You can eat it here, and when you've finished, push the wagon back to the dining-room and then go upstairs. Good night!"

Hilary had reached the door again when she heard the twins' voices.

" I say, Hilary—thanks for the supper!"

" Yes, thanks, Hilary!"

The new prefect gave them a smile over her shoulder, and left them to their supper, and for a few moments they were unusually silent, munching biscuits and sipping cocoa.

" It was decent of her," Maureen admitted at last.

" She's trying to curry favour with us, I suppose," said Madge. " We mustn't give in to her, though—we've got to be loyal to Betty and the rest. Don't forget good old Betty is giving us a chance to play for the Third to-morrow!"

" Rather not!" cried Maureen fervently.

On the whole, the juniors were rather doubtful whether the result of this first skirmish with the new prefect was one up to them, or one up to Hilary!

CHAPTER III

The Twins Hatch a Plot

Windmill School hockey field was a very pleasant place, bordered at one end by tall elms in which rooks cawed and flapped and at the other by two enormous old oaks, between which the gables of the school buildings could be glimpsed.

Memories of hard-fought battles on that field lingered in the minds of many an old Windmill girl who had left her school days far behind her.

There were two pitches, and on the farthest of these a game was in progress between the Third Eleven and a mixed team of seniors and juniors. Betty was refereeing. She was a very keen hockey captain, always on the look-out to find and encourage talent amongst the juniors.

Up till now it had been a ding-dong game, and with ten minutes to go, the score was two all.

Flushed and excited, Madge and Maureen were working like small Trojans on the Third's left wing, their " pep " and energy making up for what they lacked as yet in skill. Betty's keen eye, however, had already discerned the makings of two very fine players in the Terrible Twins. The twins worked well together, and each was beginning to show a knack of guessing just what the other was going to do.

Maureen had the ball now, and was speeding down the wing, two opposing players vainly trying to catch her. With a flick of her stick she sent the ball skimming to Madge, who was immediately tackled by the enemy centre-half, but somehow or other the ball shot out towards the wing again and Maureen pounced on it like a hawk. There was another swift advance, another swing of Maureen's stick, and the ball was centred, just within the striking circle, and almost before anyone knew it was there, Madge had banged it into the goal.

" Well played, you two!" cried Betty.

Never did praise fall more sweetly in anyone's ears, and the twins turned grateful glances towards the hockey captain, their flushed faces growing an even deeper red. Madge and Maureen snatched up praise from Betty as a dog snatches up a bone. Betty was their heroine; their one aim and hope in life was to become as like Betty as they could.

A few minutes later the game came to an end, with a win for the Third by three goals to two. Strolling off the field, Betty found the twins following close behind her.

" I say, Betty!"

" Oh, hullo, you two! I didn't know you were there," replied Betty, rather absently.

" D'you think, Betty, if we practise and practise for years and years we shall ever be able to play hockey as well as you?" demanded Maureen.

Betty laughed.

" You'll be miles better than me, I dare say, if you stick to the game and play it for all you're worth," she answered.

The twins exchanged rapturous glances. Yet they did not fail to notice the absent, troubled look on Betty's face, and they were well aware of the cause. This Betty, whom they now trotted after like a pair of loyal dogs, was not quite like the old happy, care-free Betty, and of course it was all due to the changes in Windmill, to the new head and the new prefect.

Madge and Maureen ached to show their sympathy. Madge's glance fell on the school clock tower, and this suggested one of the effects of the new tyranny.

" Isn't it beastly having to get up at seven instead of eight, Betty?" she said. " Why couldn't Miss Shephard have kept to the old time, like it was in Prissy's days?"

Before this fatal term Betty would never have dreamed of discussing or criticizing a head mistress before two mischievous juniors, but she could not keep back a bitter reply, spoken more to herself than to Madge and Maureen.

" That's not the worst of the changes."

Madge, however, was still following a train of thought suggested by the clock.

" You know, Betty, Old Andy always rings the getting-up bell, and he goes by the school clock, because he hasn't got one of his own. Wouldn't it be a lark to climb up to the clock tower one night and put the hands back an hour, so that we got up according to the old time after all. That would show Miss Shephard what we think of her rotten old ideas, wouldn't it?"

" I should think it jolly well would!" Betty

replied, without paying much attention to what Madge had said. " But now run along to your changing-room, kiddies," she added, " or you'll be late for tea."

Betty swung on her way, and with shining eyes Madge seized her twin's arm.

" We'll do it!" she breathed.

" Alter the clock, d'you mean?"

" Yes! Didn't you hear Betty say it would serve Miss Shephard right! It's something we can do to show we're loyal to Betty and the old prefects—and oh jiminy, what an adventure it will be!"

Maureen still looked doubtful.

" Your ideas sound all right," she began, " but I don't see——"

" You don't see because you haven't got enough brains to see, you old snail-coach!" retorted Madge impatiently.

" I've got as much brain as you have, slug!"

" You haven't, snail!"

" I beat you in history!"

" And I beat you in maths and—— But oh, don't let's argue about it now," went on Madge, cooling down. " This is too jolly important for squabbling, Maureen. Are you going to help me or not?"

" Of course I'll help you," replied her twin.
" Don't we do everything together? When
are we going to do it?"

Once she had got a scheme in her mind,
Madge was not one to hesitate or delay.

" To-night," she replied promptly. " There'll
be a moon, and that will help us, but, of course,
we'll have to wait till everyone is in bed and
asleep."

" We could get up to the roof through the
skylight in the lumber attic," suggested Maureen
helpfully.

" Good for you, kid! But I say, I've thought
of something. If we put the clock back an
hour, shan't we make the striking wrong?
That might spoil everything."

The Terrible Twins knitted their brows in
thought.

" I've got it!" said Madge at last. " Suppose we alter the hands at midnight. Well,
we must be ready to move them at a minute
to twelve, before it strikes, and we must put
them so they point to a minute past eleven.
That won't interfere with the striking at
all."

The more they thought about their daring
plan, the more thrilled the twins became.

Not a word did they breathe to their companions of the junior school, but it was noted that they both ate tremendous teas. Midnight adventurers, of course, must keep their strength up!

CHAPTER IV

Midnight on the Roof

Dim rays of moonlight filtered through the diamond-paned windows of Squirrel Dormitory, showing up the nine little white beds in which seven juniors were fast asleep. It was some time since the school clock had struck eleven, and all was quiet except for the faint snoring of Isabel Bayley, whose sleep was troubled by dreams in which William of Orange was being pursued by seven enormous hungry cats.

At the far end of the room was the cubicle in which the prefect in charge of the dormitory should have been sleeping. The cubicle was now empty, and would remain so till Miss Shephard saw fit to appoint new prefects in place of those who had resigned.

There were three junior dormitories at Windmill, known as the Squirrel, the Penguin and the Bear, the walls of each decorated with the animal or bird from which it took its name.

Hilary Day was in charge of Penguin Dorm, but the other two had no prefect at present.

Suddenly the peace of Squirrel Dorm was disturbed by two small figures sitting up in the two end beds. One glance they gave each other, then clambered silently out of bed, stooping to don slippers and quickly wrapping dressing-gowns round their neat blue sleeping-suits.

Like conspirators in some old-time plot they stole to the door; the handle gave the faintest of clicks as one of them opened it, and they passed out, leaving the other occupants of Squirrel Dorm sleeping undisturbed.

" So far, so good!" murmured Madge.

Maureen nodded, and silently they pursued their way up the corridor, till they reached the narrow staircase leading to the big attic. Without a pause, their hearts beating fast, they crept upwards, Madge switching on the electric torch she had brought with her.

How ghostly the beam of light looked, shifting to and fro and producing weird shadows on walls and ceiling! A stair creaked, and Maureen gave a little gasp.

" Hush, idiot!" breathed Madge.

The twins stood clutching each other for a moment or two, but all was quiet below. That creaking board, which had sounded so loud to them, had evidently not roused the school!

Once again they commenced their upward climb, breathing more freely when the attic door was reached; there was not so much chance now that any faint sounds they might make would be heard downstairs. A few seconds later they stood inside the long attic, the door safely closed behind them.

Something scuttled across the floor, and Maureen nearly screamed.

" Ow! A mouse!" she wailed. " I can't stand mice, Madge. I don't mind the roof, or the clock, but—mice!"

" Then go back," said Madge calmly, directing her torch on the skylight.

" I won't go back! This is just as much my plan as yours!"

" Who said it wasn't, fathead? Look, we'll have to pile boxes under the skylight, so we can get through."

The skylight was a large one, with a sliding pane that would leave a fair-sized opening. There were plenty of empty trunks and boxes in the attic, and Maureen tried to forget mice and set to work to help her twin erect a kind of pyramid under the skylight. Both girls were

good at gym and very active, and they had no
qualms as they faced the feat of climbing that
was needed to carry out their plan.

Madge went first. The skylight was close to
the peak of the roof, and when she had squeezed
through she was able to grasp the curved tiles
at the top and pull herself up till she was
sitting astride them, with the steeply sloping
roof dropping away on either hand. If one
started slipping or sliding down that slope, one
might have to face the thirty-foot drop beyond
the guttering at the edge.

Madge shivered a little, wrapping her dressing-gown more tightly round her, and leaning
down to give her twin a hand. Soon they were
both seated astride the top of the roof, the chill
breeze stirring their hair.

" Forward!" whispered Madge.

In front of them, about twenty feet away,
rose the square clock tower, and their first aim
was to reach this, by edging their way slowly
along. Madge kept her eyes fixed on the tower,
and Maureen kept her gaze glued on Madge,
and both tried to forget the perilous slopes
beneath them.

Those twenty feet seemed like twenty miles,
but at last they were close to the square tower,

and the deep tick-tock of the clock sounded like a grave warning in their ears.

They were face to face now with the most dangerous part of their reckless prank. It would be necessary for one of them to stand up, balance herself on the ledge that went round the base of the tower, and work her way round till she was able to grasp the long hand of the clock and move it backwards.

The Terrible Twins did everything together as far as possible, but here was something that only one of them could accomplish. They had tossed up for it after tea, and the lot had fallen to Madge, which was perhaps lucky, for she was the cooler-headed of the two.

" For goodness sake, take care, Madge!" came Maureen's urgent whisper. " D'you think it's worth risking, after all? Suppose you fall!"

" I shan't fall, my kidlet! Trust me!"

Already Madge was standing upright, and her twin watched anxiously as the daring young adventurer stood on the ledge, her arms spread out, clasping whatever handhold the brickwork offered. A cloud drifted across the moon, and when it shone clear again Madge was edging her way round the corner of the tower.

This was very nerve-racking for Maureen, for she could not see her twin, once she had turned the corner of the tower. What was Madge doing? Was she right in front of the clock-face now? Had she grasped the long hand, and was she dragging it slowly backwards?

Snap! Thud!

Maureen's hand went to her mouth to stifle a scream of terror. Her twin had come into view again, but not perched on the ledge this time. To the watcher's horror, Madge was sliding and rolling down the steep slope of the roof, desperately clawing at the tiles but unable to stop herself, and each moment drawing nearer to the dreadful precipice at the edge.

Never in after life did Maureen forget those moments of sheer terror. She remembered the unspeakable surge of relief that welled up within her when the headlong slide was checked, within a few feet of the edge.

Madge's foot had caught in a space where a tile was missing, and she stopped there, lying full length on the roof, looking up at her twin perched at the top.

The need for silence was forgotten.

" Madge! Oh, for goodness sake don't slip

any farther! What can I do? How can I help you?"

The reply did not come at once. Madge was striving to get her breath again, and give her heart a chance to stop jumping so wildly.

" Keep as quiet as you can!" she called back at last. " I think I'm all right now, but I can't climb up without something to help me. What about the girdle of your dressing-gown?"

In a twinkling Maureen had whipped it off and let it dangle down towards her twin, but it was not nearly long enough.

" It's no good," she called hoarsely. " I'll have to fetch help, Madge—it's the only way. Don't try to climb by yourself!"

Madge made some reply, but Maureen's panic-stricken ears did not catch what it was. Wriggling round, she was frantically working her way back to the open skylight, careless of danger to herself. Never before, perhaps, had she realized what it would mean to her if " something happened " to Madge.

" Oh, please God, don't let her fall—don't let her fall!" she kept whispering.

Trembling, she lowered herself through the skylight, but in her haste she did it so clumsily that a box was dislodged, and fell to the floor with what seemed an echoing crash. Never caring for this, Maureen groped her way to the door, flung it open and stumbled down the stairs.

At the foot she came face to face with Hilary Day, standing with her hand on the electric light switch, which she had just turned on.

"Maureen! What on earth is the matter? Where have you been?"

Half sobbing, Maureen grasped Hilary's arm.

"It's Madge! She's on the roof—she slipped, and she's hanging on near the edge, and my girdle won't reach her, and—oh, *Hilary*!"

There was something very dependable about Hilary Day in a time of crisis such as this. Her cubicle in Penguin Dorm was just under the attic, and she had been roused by the noise Maureen made in scrambling through the skylight, but whatever she might have imagined as the cause of the sounds, she had certainly not expected to be confronted with a panic-stricken Maureen, telling of a girl in danger on the roof. Yet Hilary did not lose her presence of mind, and she remembered the cupboard on the landing in which certain stores were kept, amongst them lengths of cord for tying up trunks and boxes. It was the work of an instant to dart to this cupboard and bring out a length of strong cord.

" Show me how you got up to the roof, Maureen! Quick!"

Stifling her sobs, Maureen hurried up the attic stairs, with the new prefect at her heels.

" We g-got out through the skylight," she panted. " But perhaps it will be too small for you, Hilary."

Hilary was slim and agile, however, and it took her very little time to worm her way through the open skylight on to the top of the roof. The moonlight showed her that small figure, nearly at the foot of the slope below the clock tower.

" Hold on!" called Hilary. " I'm coming!"

In a surprisingly short time, Hilary had reached the tower, grasping the cord.

" I'm going to lower this cord to you," she informed Madge. " But I'd like something to tie it to first."

To her relief, she found a strong iron staple in the side of the tower, where a flagstaff had once been fixed, and she knotted one end of the cord to this, letting the other end drop down to where Madge's outstretched fingers were awaiting it.

" Are you sure you can manage?" Hilary called. " Take it slowly, Madge. Pull yourself up bit by bit."

With the aid of the cord, it was a fairly easy matter for Madge to crawl up the slope, and there was Hilary waiting to help her on to the roof-top.

" Thanks awfully, Hilary," she panted. " Where's Maureen? Is she all right?"

" She's waiting in the attic," Hilary said, untying the cord. " Don't talk now, Madge. Let's get back."

Maureen was still stifling sobs when they joined her, and she rushed at her twin, enveloping her in a bear-like hug.

" Oh, Madge, I'm so jolly glad you're safe! I wish we'd never thought of that trick of moving the clock back, don't you? It was just because Betty said it would be a good joke that we——"

" Shut up, idiot!" whispered Madge.

In her usual frame of mind Maureen would never have brought Betty's name into it at all, but she was overwrought and overtired, and the words slipped out almost before she realized it.

" Do you mean to say that Betty suggested

this mad prank?" exclaimed Hilary. " Betty Lyndon?"

Madge shook her head vigorously.

" No, no, of course she didn't, Hilary," she replied. " We thought of it ourselves. We were trying to put the clock back an hour, so we shouldn't have to keep the new rule about getting up at seven, but the ledge broke before I could move the hands. Betty had nothing to do with it at all."

" But you mentioned it to her?" questioned Hilary.

Madge wriggled.

" Well, sort of," she confessed. " But she didn't know we were really going to do it. It was our own idea—really it was. I say, Hilary, are you going to report us?"

Hilary stared at them thoughtfully.

" I suppose I ought to," she said. " It was a senseless, crazy prank, and it might have had a terrible ending. But I should think you've been punished enough by the fright you've had. Promise me you'll never, never go on the roof again."

" Yes, we promise, Hilary," replied the twins solemnly.

" Very well, we'll say no more about it,"

agreed Hilary. " And if I were you, I wouldn't talk about it to the others. Now creep back to bed, kiddies, and let's hope you haven't caught cold."

Hilary went with them to the corridor below, and they were turning to go, when a sudden impulse seized Maureen. She ran to Hilary and, standing on tiptoe, kissed her cheek.

" That's for saving Madge!" she whispered.

Perhaps the strain had told on Hilary more than she knew, for her eyes were blurred as she watched the twins creep softly away to their dormitory.

Yet, as she walked to her own room, Hilary was not thinking of the twins. Her thoughts were of Betty Lyndon.

From the rather confused story which Madge and Maureen had told, Hilary gathered that Betty had a definite responsibility for the dangerous prank on which the twins had embarked that night. They had done it because they thought Betty would approve of it, and they had even spoken of it to Betty beforehand.

" And she didn't try to stop them!" Hilary said to herself. " She was glad to vent her spite on Auntie through the twins!"

The more she thought of it, the more coldly

angry did Hilary become. To her duty-loving mind, it seemed a terrible thing that a senior should have condoned such a prank, should actually have encouraged it!

" They're sporting kiddies, and they tried to shield Betty, of course," Hilary's thoughts ran on. " Her name only slipped out by accident. I'd never have believed it of her!"

Before she went to sleep again, Hilary came to a decision.

" I won't report the twins," she told herself. " But I'm going to tax Betty with this to-morrow. It's my duty to have it out with her face to face. How could she? How *could* she?"

CHAPTER V

A Quarrel

" I wonder why Prissy hasn't written? I wonder *why*?"

This was the question Betty was asking herself, over and over again, as she sat in Study 3, a book lying forgotten on her lap. Afternoon school was over, and through the window floated the voices and footsteps of girls walking and talking in the courtyard.

Betty was deaf to such sounds, however, and though she had just lit the gas fire and was gazing at it, she hardly saw its warm yellow glow.

Betty was thinking of the last day of last term, when Miss Priscilla Jennings—her so beloved head mistress—had said good-bye to the school she had served so well. Dear, kind Prissy! Betty remembered the suffocating lump which had risen in her throat as she listened to those simple words of farewell, and how a ray of sunlight falling through the window had touched Prissy's silver hair like a good-bye caress.

Prissy had spoken, then, of the traditions and spirit of the school, and how she trusted her girls to carry them on when she had gone.

" And I will, too," Betty had vowed, almost fiercely. " I'll fight for the things Prissy loved, just as if she were here."

It is necessary to go back several years to find the beginning of Betty's loyalty and love. Betty's father was in India, and she had no mother. How vividly she recalled that bleak November day, three years ago, when news had come that her mother had been killed in a railway accident, and that henceforth there would be no " mums dear " to write to and look forward to seeing any more!

It was Prissy who had broken the news to the wild-eyed, pale-faced thirteen-year-old girl, and it was she who had been so gentle and understanding that she had almost taken the place of the mother Betty had lost. Never could Betty speak of these things to anyone else, never could she describe what Prissy's kindness had meant to her in her time of trouble and ever since. It was all printed on Betty's heart, and a true friendship had sprung up between the schoolgirl and the mistress.

Betty had been forced to spend several holidays at school, and the link between her and Prissy had been strengthened by long walks and talks about the countryside.

Sometimes Miss Jennings had spoken of the time when she would retire from her post at the head of Windmill School. Once they had clambered up the steep slopes of Beacon Hill, and Prissy had pointed to a little white house which could just be seen nestling in the valley two miles beyond.

" When my time of rest comes I shall live there," she had smiled. " There will always be a welcome for you there, Betty, my dear. I trust our friendship will always keep bright."

We can understand why Betty felt the changes that were coming to Windmill more keenly than the other girls. Perhaps she was misguided and wrong, but she could not help regarding Miss Shephard as an interloper who had taken Prissy's place. Every change was regarded by Betty as an act of disloyalty to Prissy's memory.

Perhaps it would not have been so bad if her old friend had only written. Miss Jennings had settled, as Betty supposed, in the little white house away in the distance beyond

Beacon Hill. Betty had written to her there, but no reply had come.

Betty had even hoped that there might be week-ends when Prissy would invite her to spend some little time at the white house, and how good it would have been just to see Prissy again, and to hear her voice! Betty would have poured out her troubles, and Prissy would have spoken words of kindly wisdom that would have made things smooth and straight again.

What was the meaning of her friend's strange silence?

It certainly had the effect of making Betty still more troubled and unhappy during the opening of this new term. It made her even fiercer in her vows of loyalty to Prissy. Let Prissy keep silence, if she would, it would make no difference to Betty's loyal heart.

A tap at the door suddenly broke in on Betty's dreams.

" Come in!"

Turning her head, she saw it was Hilary Day who had entered the study. A wave of hostility ran through Betty. It seemed as if this new girl, with her cool grey eyes, represented everything that was making Betty so anxious and troubled.

" Oh, hullo," she said coldly.

" I want to speak to you, Betty. It's something rather serious."

There was a slight tremble in Hilary's voice. It was not an easy matter for her to face Betty in her own den, so to speak, though her sense of duty was forcing her to carry it through.

" Fire away!" responded Betty, picking up her book as if anxious to continue her reading.

Betty was not even looking at Hilary. She seemed quite indifferent as to whether the new prefect stayed or went.

" I want to know if you knew about that mad prank that Madge and Maureen tried to carry through last night," said Hilary, with an effort. " They didn't give you away, but from something that was said I got the idea that you knew about it beforehand."

Betty looked up in genuine amazement.

" What on earth are you talking about?"

" As I say, they didn't mean to mention your name," went on Hilary, striving to be fair to the twins. " They had some reckless idea of putting the clock back, so that we should get up an hour later. I thought you ought to know that Madge almost lost her life on the roof, and if you really encouraged them to do it—

if you knew beforehand and didn't try to stop them—then I think you were wicked and mean and wrong!"

The words came tumbling out of Hilary, and then she stopped, panting slightly. Well, she had said her say. She had said what it was her plain duty to say.

Betty jumped to her feet, throwing her book on the table with a thump.

" You dare!" she burst out. " You dare to come in here preaching at me, and accusing me. Get out of here! Go away!"

But Hilary stood her ground.

" If you really say you knew nothing whatever about it, then I'll apologize," she said steadily.

A teasing imp of memory began to worry the back of Betty's mind. Had the twins said something about it as they trotted at her heels after hockey yesterday? Certain words that Madge had spoken were beginning to creep into her memory, though her thoughts had been elsewhere at the time and she had not really been listening. . . .

However it might be, Betty was in no mood to search her memory just then. Hot with indignation, she faced the new prefect.

" If you think I'm going to take the trouble to explain myself to you, you're jolly well mistaken," she burst out. " I don't care what you think, or what you suspect; it just doesn't worry me in the least."

Angry brown eyes met cool grey ones.

" I thought it was only fair to tell you what I felt," Hilary said. " It shows that, if you encourage juniors to break rules, it may lead to——"

" But I tell you, I've never encouraged juniors to break rules!" cried Betty. " I hate the new system here, and I've made no secret of it amongst the seniors, but I——"

Again that teasing imp of memory checked Betty. Was there really a glimmer of truth in what Hilary was saying? Of course, she had never encouraged the twins to play that risky prank, she had never dreamed they would do it; but she had vaguely heard what they said as they left the hockey field. Hadn't she agreed that it would be a good joke if someone were to do it?

To cover up these pangs of conscience, Betty spoke with growing bitterness.

" Why come to me about it, anyway?" she went on. " If you think I've done such terrible wrong, why not trot along and tell the head? She brought you here to spy on us, and I should think she'd be glad——"

The grey eyes were angry now.

" That's a lie, Betty! I've never spied on anyone in my life."

" Everyone thinks that's what you're here for."

" I don't care what they think!" cried Hilary. " You're all upset because Miss Shephard wants to change some of your old-fashioned ways. You never stop to think that perhaps Miss Shephard may know better in some things than your old head mistress."

" She couldn't—she couldn't know better than Prissy!" burst out Betty, so fiercely that Hilary was startled. " I warn you, I won't hear a word against Prissy from you—not one word!"

So excited had Betty become that she seized Hilary's shoulders and began to push her towards the door, which at that moment opened suddenly to disclose Sonia Starforth.

Wrapped in dreams of her glorious ancestry, Sonia had the habit of entering other people's studies without warning. Open-mouthed, she stood gazing at the angry girls.

" Oh, I say, I'm sorry, Betty," she gasped. " I didn't know you had someone here."

" It's all right, I'm going," Hilary said.

She disengaged herself from Betty's grasp and then, resuming something of her usual calm, strolled past Sonia into the corridor.

" The priggish little spy!" Sonia heard Betty whisper, with trembling lips.

Turning, Betty strode to the window and stood looking out, her back to Sonia, apparently unaware that Sonia was still there.

" I say, Betty," began Sonia. " I've just brought a cutting from our local paper at home that Mother sent me. It's an article by the vicar—he's a great student of history, you know. He has been searching the records, and he finds that it was my ancestor, Sir Stilyard Starforth, who struck the first blow in the Battle of Sedgemoor. On the king's side, of course, for we Starforths have always been loyal to the throne."

Sonia paused, but no comment came from Betty, and there was something about that rigid figure at the window that warned the visitor that she was unheeded.

" Oh, well, if you don't want to hear, then I'll go," Sonia said.

Still no word came from Betty, and with a
toss of her head Sonia withdrew. It was not
long before she was relating to a group of girls
how she had surprised Hilary and Betty in a
most desperate quarrel.

Sonia's story lost nothing in the telling, and
as it spread from mouth to mouth the quarrel
took on even more alarming proportions. It
was plain to everyone that Hilary and Betty
were at daggers drawn. One account went so
far as to state that, when Sonia entered the
study, Betty was grasping a heavy inkpot and
Hilary had snatched up a ruler, and it was only
Sonia's presence of mind in rushing between
them that prevented a mortal combat from
starting!

In the junior play-room everyone was agog
with the news.

" Can't you think of some new wheeze for
ragging Hilary, twins, to show we're on Betty's
side?" asked Lorna Wood.

To everyone's amazement, the Terrible Twins
shook their heads.

" We're not ragging Hilary any more,"
announced Madge.

" No, we're jolly well not," agreed Maureen.
No wonder the juniors stared!

" And what's more, if we catch any of you ragging Hilary, we'll knock your heads together," threatened Madge.

" And pull your hair!" added Maureen.

Knowing nothing of last night's adventure on the roof, the juniors were quite at a loss to explain this sudden change. Up till now, the Terrible Twins had been foremost in ideas for ragging the new prefect. Why had they suddenly switched over to Hilary's side? What did it mean?

They could not find an answer to the puzzle.

Only little Isabel Bayley—that queer solitary child—was unmoved by these strange happenings. She was always slipping away from the others on mysterious errands of her own, and it was generally agreed that she had a new pet stowed away somewhere.

" If all the seniors were fighting hammer and tongs, Isabel would only be thinking of her pets," said Lorna. " She's hopeless!"

CHAPTER VI

Who Ragged Hilary's Study?

Under the south wall were tiny plots reserved for the use of juniors who had a taste for gardening, and in one of these Madge and Maureen found another outlet for their energies. It was also the cause of many a heated argument.

" I tell you we ought to cut the rose-tree, Maureen. It's all wispy and straggly."

" Prune it, you mean!"

" No, I don't, you fathead! Prunes are things you eat with custard, and I don't like them, though matron says they're awfully good for you."

Maureen went into fits of laughter at her twin's ignorance.

" You are a scream, Madge, you little worm! I tell you, pruning is the right word, and the proper time to do it is the spring, not the autumn. Miss Battle told me so."

(Miss Battle was games mistress, drill mistress, and general overseer of the junior gardens.)

"Pooh! Miss Battle may know a lot about P.T., but she doesn't know a thing about roses. . . ."

Suddenly Madge's eye was caught by their clump of chrysanthemums, a lovely cluster of bronze blooms.

"I say, what are we going to do with those?" she said thoughtfully, changing the subject with a suddenness that was quite typical of the twins' debates.

Hitherto there had been no doubt in the twins' minds as to what to do with any bunch of flowers they might gather. They were given as an offering to their heroine, Betty, and graced the table of Study 3.

But now they paused to think. Of course, Betty was still their idol, and they would have been very angry if anyone had dared to deny it, and yet something had happened to divide their feelings.

They could not forget the prompt and plucky way in which Hilary had rescued Madge on that fateful night of roof-climbing. Still more, they were eternally grateful to Hilary for not reporting them. Never again would they rag

Hilary, and when they had heard the lurid reports of the quarrel between the two seniors, they had not been able to prevent their sympathies veering away from Betty towards the new prefect.

So they stared at the bronze flowers trembling gently in the breeze, and at last Madge said:

" I think we might give the whole bunch to Hilary. After all, we've never given her anything to show how grateful we are to her."

" All right," agreed Madge. " Let's take them to her now."

Five minutes later they were hurrying towards the school buildings with the bunch of flowers, and they were seen by Betty and Esme Randall, who were strolling beside the tennis courts.

" More flowers for your study, Betty!" drawled Esme. " I wish I had the knack of getting myself worshipped by the juniors, as you seem to do. I suppose it's your hockey that does it. Ugh! How I hate hockey!"

Betty laughed lightly, but all the same, it was rather nice to feel that you were regarded as a heroine by a pair of eager youngsters like Madge and Maureen.

" I'm afraid they'll find nobody there, if they

call at the study," she smiled. " But if the flowers are for me, I expect they'll leave them. And now, Esme, about this new cranky idea of Miss Shephard's . . ."

Esme sighed.

" Dear old Betty!" she thought. " She's beginning to be a bit of a bore with her eternal plans for rebelling against the head. We've resigned our prefectships. What on earth more can we do?"

To tell the truth, Esme's artistic soul was missing the privileges that went with being a prefect, especially the extra half-holiday once a fortnight, which was so useful for sketching and painting out of doors. She was heartily wishing she had never allowed Betty to rush her into resigning like that.

Before they knew where they were, Miss Shephard would decide to appoint new prefects, and they would lose their chances for good and all. However, Betty was eagerly pouring out her protests and her plans, and with a shrug of her shoulders Esme pretended to listen and to agree.

Meanwhile, the twins were at Hilary's door.

" How about hanging them on the door knob and creeping away?" suggested Maureen, suddenly shy. " She'll guess who they come from. We're the only ones who've got chrysanths like this."

Madge nodded, and they were in the very act of tying them on, when a cool, clear voice spoke behind them.

" Hullo! What are you two kiddies doing? Oh, what gorgeous flowers! Are they really for me?"

" Yes, they're for you, Hilary," Madge blurted out. " We—I——"

She was trying to say that the flowers were a little thank-offering for what Hilary had done for them, but somehow the words failed her.

" You must come in and help me find a vase for them," smiled the new prefect. " How ever did you guess that that lovely bronzy tint is my favourite colour?"

As she spoke, Hilary threw open the door, and they stepped inside, all three of them halting in amazement just within the study.

The room was in utter confusion. Books were strewn on the floor, chairs were overturned, and the inkpot had been upset, spilling a glistening black pool on the table cloth. Every picture had been turned face to the wall, every photo had been thrown down.

Hilary's gaze went to a shelf near the window, on which had stood a little porcelain figure of a dancing girl. She drew in her breath sharply as she saw that it lay on the floor, broken into several pieces.

In awe-struck silence Madge and Maureen stared at the scene, eyes and mouths wide open. Not a word came from Hilary as she stepped across the littered floor and picked up the fragments of porcelain, holding them in her hand.

Surely the person who had ragged the study could not have known that this ornament was a special favourite of Hilary's. It had been given to her by an uncle before he sailed away to the other side of the world, and the lightness and grace of the porcelain figure had always found an echo in Hilary's heart. Now here it lay, brutally smashed.

One shining tear dropped on to the porcelain fragments that lay in Hilary's hand.

The watchful twins saw the tear, and lumps rose to their own throats. Turning away, they at once began to talk loudly, as if to assure Hilary that never, never had they noticed that she was crying.

" What an awful shame!" burst out Madge.

" Who could have done it?" wondered Maureen. " We don't rag people's studies at Windmill. At least, I've never heard of it being done!"

" Let's help you clear up the mess, Hilary!" said Madge.

" Oh yes, do let's!" echoed Maureen.

Eagerly they began to pick up photos and books, and by this time Hilary had regained something of her normal calm.

" Thanks, twins," she said, striving to keep her voice steady. " I should be grateful for a little help. I can't imagine who did it, but whoever it was, they seem to have made a good job of it."

Did they really hate her as much as that? Hilary was thinking. Betty had called her a spy, and perhaps that was what some of the others thought too. Perhaps that was what nearly all of them thought, and they had agreed to rag her study to show her how unpopular she was! And she had been foolish enough to think that, bit by bit, she might win them over.

Maureen swung round suddenly, her arms full of books.

" Oh, my goodness, I hope you don't think

we did it, Hilary!" she cried, as the dreadful possibility dawned on her. " We were close to the door when you came along, you know!"

Hilary summoned up a laugh.

" My dear child, of course I don't," she replied. " When one rags someone's study, one doesn't usually leave bunches of flowers on the door knob. I know you both well enough to be quite sure you'd never do anything mean or underhand or—or cruel," she added.

It was just then that Madge, stooping down by the hearth, noticed a scrap of paper lying there, with a few words printed roughly on it in pencil. Maureen and Hilary had their backs turned, so they did not see the way Madge's face wrinkled up in dismay as she read those pencilled words.

For a moment Madge hesitated, then quick as a flash she seized the paper and pushed it into the pocket of her tunic, out of sight.

Maureen was still chattering away, giving out a score of theories as to who could have committed this outrage (her latest idea was that it had been done by passing gipsies!). But Madge did not join in the talk, and was as silent as Hilary herself.

" There! How's that?" exclaimed Maureen

at last, proudly surveying the result of their work.

The ink had been mopped up, pictures and photos put to rights, and the litter on the floor cleared away, so that the study looked almost as spick-and-span as usual.

" Yes, it looks more like home now, doesn't it?" said Hilary, with a faint smile. " I'm terribly grateful to you, twins." Her glance fell on the bunch of chrysanthemums lying neglected on a chair. " My goodness, we mustn't forget those!" she went on. " It's lucky that vase by the window wasn't broken as well, and I think that will be the best place for them."

The tireless Maureen dashed away to fill the vase with water, and Hilary waited quietly by the window, seemingly unaware that Madge was waiting with her. Madge wondered what was passing in Hilary's mind, and if she had been hurt very much by this crude practical joke.

Madge's fingers strayed to her pocket, as if on the point of taking out the paper and showing it to Hilary, but then she shook her head slightly and her hand dropped to her side again.

They had only a minute to wait, and Maureen was back again, the vase filled.

" Shall I put it here by the window, Hilary?"
she asked.

" Yes, please. And do stay and help me
arrange the flowers," was Hilary's reply, as the
vase was placed on the broad window-sill.

The three of them were bending over it together, arranging the lovely autumn blooms,
when Betty Lyndon and Esme passed on the
gravel walk outside. The high-pitched voices
of the twins could not fail to reach Betty's ears,
and she turned her head and saw the little
group around the flower-vase. At that moment
Madge happened to look up, and her eyes met
Betty's for an instant.

Betty's cheeks flamed suddenly red, and she
made haste to look the other way, angry with
herself for feeling so hurt.

Yes, she was hurt—she could not deny it.
She had made so sure that those bronze blooms
were for her; for had not the twins again and
again offered her their loyal gifts as proofs of
devotion? And now they had taken them to
Hilary, of all people! To the new prefect, who
stood for all that Betty was fighting against!

Of course, it was absurd to bother her head
about a pair of irresponsible juniors like Madge
and Maureen, and yet Betty could not help

feeling as if a prop had suddenly given way beneath her. By what arts and crafts had Hilary won the twins over?

" Dear me, we are bad prophets, Betty, my child," put in Esme's drawling voice. " The flowers have gone elsewhere, it seems. Quite a pretty group they made in the window, don't you think?"

Betty laughed. She did not intend to let Esme know how she felt.

" You ought to paint them, Esme," she replied lightly. " You might manage the twins and Hilary, but honestly I doubt if you could paint those chrysanths—they're too gorgeous. Well, I must fly!"

Tossing her brown hair, Betty hurried away, leaving Esme to shrug her shoulders and smile a slow smile.

The twins were leaving Hilary's study arm-in-arm. At the end of the corridor they encountered Isabel Bayley—that solitary child— who stared at them in a panic-stricken manner, as if afraid that they had designs on William of Orange, or the silkworms, or some other of her outlandish pets.

However, no one took much notice of Isabel, and the twins hurried on their way, Madge guiding her sister to a quiet corner where they could talk unobserved. Here, for the first time, Maureen became aware that her twin was labouring under a sense of excitement.

" Do you know what I found in Hilary's study?" Madge breathed.

" Haven't the foggiest. What?"

" This!"

Out came the crumpled scrap of paper, and Maureen scanned the roughly printed words:

" *Serves you right.—B. L.*"

At first, Maureen scarcely understood what it meant.

" Don't you see, silly? It was left by the person who ragged Hilary's study. Those are her initials at the end—B. L."

" Then why didn't you give it to Hilary?" inquired Maureen.

" Because it suddenly flashed on me what those initials stood for. I've been over all the names in the school, and there's only one with those initials—I'm sure of it. B. L. Think, Maureen!"

Maureen thought, and her eyes opened wide.

" You don't mean—Betty Lyndon? Oh, but she'd never dream of doing a thing like that. She couldn't!"

Madge pursed her lips.

" That's what I'd have thought," she agreed. " But those are her initials, sure enough. And you know she had a terrible quarrel with Hilary not long ago, and she's ever so bitter against Hilary and the new head. Everybody knows it. That seems to prove it, you know—and there's something else besides."

Awe-struck, Maureen was drinking it all in.

" I happened to see Betty while we were arranging the flowers in Hilary's window," Madge said. " And when she caught my eye she went as red as fire. Honest, she did! Doesn't that mean that she's got a guilty— guilty—what's the word——?"

" Conscience," suggested Maureen.

" That's it. She had a guilty conscience because she knew she had ragged the study, and that was why she turned so red."

The twins were silent. Almost one could hear the clatter of the idol falling from its pedestal — their idol, Betty Lyndon, whose slightest word of praise, such a little while ago, had given them the keenest delight.

The twins were very impulsive, very liable to be carried away by new ideas. They were becoming quite convinced that it was Betty who had ragged Hilary's study because she had quarrelled with her, and disliked her, and wanted to get her own back.

They remembered the tear that had dropped on the porcelain fragments, and all their warm sympathies centred on Hilary.

" But why didn't you show the paper to Hilary?" Maureen repeated the question she had asked before.

" Because I was scared to. I was afraid Hilary might report Betty to the head, and she'd get expelled or something dreadful like that. It was an awfully rotten thing to do, but somehow I couldn't bring myself to show the paper to Hilary."

" It would certainly be awful if Betty got expelled," agreed Maureen, who, like her twin, was a trifle hazy about the type of crime for which one got expelled from school. " All the same, it doesn't seem fair that Betty should get off scot-free. Shall we rag Betty's study in revenge?"

Madge shook her head.

" Don't you remember Hilary said we were not the sort to do things like that?" she replied. " I tell you what we'll do, though. We'll send Betty to Coventry."

" I say! That's pretty stiff. Can you do that to a prefect?"

" She isn't a prefect, stupid, since she resigned. She's only an ordinary senior. We'll send her to Coventry, and we'll make the other kids do the same, though we won't tell them exactly why."

Along the end of the corridor drifted the solitary form of Isabel Bayley.

" There's Isabel, mooning about!" cried Madge. " Let's chase her, and make her show us William of Orange. Come on!"

Forgetting these anxious problems and throwing dull care to the winds, the twins raced away.

CHAPTER VII

A Hockey Match—and After

There was one hockey fixture which always caused a great deal of interest during the autumn term, and that was the match with Cliff College. It was an " away " match this year, and never yet had Windmill School beaten the college on their own ground.

Since she had become hockey captain, one of Betty's great ambitions was to break this chain of defeats, and she and her team were full of hope and determination as they caught the train for Clifftown on the Saturday following the ragging of Hilary's study.

With them went Miss Battle and a few privileged seniors, including Esme Randall, who was bemoaning her own folly in going to watch a hockey match when she might have been out sketching.

" I only hope dear Sonia doesn't score a goal," she drawled. " If she does, it will be sure to remind her of something one of her ancestors did at the Battle of Crécy, and the whole game will have to stop while she tells everyone about it!"

" Considering Sonia is our goal-keeper, it isn't very likely that she'll score, Esme!" retorted Mary Towle. " That just shows how little you know about the team."

" My dear child, I know nothing whatever about it," said Esme. " I'm interested in art, not in hockey."

Esme was evidently in one of her very superior and tantalizing moods!

" I wonder you don't travel first-class, Esme," laughed Hilda Field. " It must be dreadful for you to have to mix with common hockey-playing girls like us!"

" It's a good thing Miss Battle isn't in this compartment, or you'd get one of her terrific snubs, Esme, my child!" smiled Betty.

Hilda changed the subject by asking if Hilary Day was coming to watch the game, but it appeared that Hilary, as the only prefect, was taking Miss Battle's place at Windmill this afternoon, and supervising the junior games.

" Aha! I expect she is winning some more of the juniors over to her side," drawled Esme, with a sidelong glance at Betty from her lazy blue eyes. "You know, Betty, as we're all supposed to be up in arms against the new head, I wonder you don't try to lose matches, instead of winning them—just to spite Miss Shephard."

Betty flushed. How hateful Esme could be, when she was in that teasing mood of hers!

"Don't be ridiculous!" Betty said. "Upon my word, Esme, if you've only come to crab and sneer, I wish you'd stayed behind. We shall jolly well want all the encouragement we can get this afternoon."

"Hear, hear!" cried Mary.

Peering out of the window, Sonia announced that she could see the roofs of Cliff College in the distance. It was only a ten-mile journey, and the girls jumped to their feet, reaching for hockey bags and other belongings on the racks.

Miss Battle had the tickets, and she was soon marshalling her little crowd on the platform, where several of the friendly Cliff girls had come to greet their foes.

" They seem to grow specially big and hefty girls at Cliff," whispered Hilda. "They look as if they are quite sure they're going to beat us again!"

" No fight is lost till the last shot has been

fired," put in Sonia. " That's what my ancestor, Sir Stopforth Starforth, used to say, and you needn't grin like that, Esme, even if you are sore because you haven't got any ancestors of your own!"

The match was due to start at three, and a few minutes before the hour the teams strolled out on to the field, the Windmill girls in brown tunics and the Cliff girls in blue.

A big crowd of girls and friends had gathered to support the home team, and already they were shouting their encouragement with all the force of lusty young throats.

" Cliff! Come on, Cliff!"

" This will make the fifteenth win, Cliff! Keep it up!"

Yes, it was quite true. Fourteen times had Windmill been beaten on the Cliff ground, and never a single victory or even a draw to their credit.

" *Windmi-i-ill!*"

Luckily Miss Battle had a voice like the note of a trumpet, and she was raising it now, the other Windmill girls joining in. Even Esme, in spite of herself, caught some of the enthusiasm!

Taking her place at centre-forward, Betty

gazed around the field, giving a swift backward glance to see that all her players were in position. This was her last year at Windmill, so it would be the last chance she would have of turning all those defeats into victory.

The whistle blew, shrill and sharp, and Betty clashed sticks with the rival captain, and a moment later the ball was spinning out to the wing.

The Cliff right-winger was a lean, lanky girl who could run like an ostrich, and almost before the Windmill team had gathered themselves together, she was scooting down the field, the other Cliff forwards never losing touch with her.

Bang! The ball was cleverly centred, and the Cliff inside-right sent it whizzing into the corner of the goal, in spite of Sonia's frantic effort to save.

A goal within the first minute of the match! No wonder a hurricane of cheering rose up from the watching ranks of Cliff girls, many of whom were predicting that the match would be an absolute walk-over this year.

" Hard luck, Windmill!" came Miss Battle's ringing shout. " Better luck next time!"

Betty waved her hand and laughed, for like

a good captain she would not let her team see that she was downhearted.

" Mark that lanky girl," she whispered. " For goodness sake don't let her get away again."

Once more the whistle blew, but the Cliff team could make no more of their lightning rushes just at present, and if the lean right-winger tried to break away, she was immediately tackled and her way was blocked.

To and fro the battle waged. Once Hilda shot for goal, but the ball hit the post and bounced behind the line. A few moments later the tide of war had flowed back into the Windmill half, and Sonia was called on to make several brilliant saves.

" Good old Sonia! Well saved indeed!"

Surely it was not Esme's voice! Yes, the most artistic girl in Windmill, caught up in the general excitement, was shouting herself hoarse with the rest of them.

But even Sonia could not perform miracles. A little before the end of the first half there came two shots in quick succession. Sonia stopped the first one, but could not hit it clear, and a swift stroke from the Cliff captain returned the ball, and this time it entered the net.

Two goals to nil! The hurricane of cheering from the Cliff supporters seemed as if sounding the knell of Windmill hopes.

That was the position at half-time, when lemons and lumps of sugar were brought out for the panting, breathless girls. During the welcome rest, Miss Battle strolled across for a word with Betty.

" Attack, my dear!" she said. " That must be your watchword for the rest of the game. Attack—attack—attack! It's the only chance."

Betty nodded, tossing back the brown hair from her forehead in the gesture her friends knew so well.

The second half of that match has taken its place in Windmill hockey history, and girls who saw it are fond of describing the scene. They speak, first of all, of that amazing run of Betty's, soon after the whistle sounded, when she took possession of the ball and threaded her way through all opposition, seeming to bear a charmed life, till she scored with a shot so swift that the Cliff goal-keeper never even saw it!

They will speak next of the enormous cheer that Miss Battle and the half-dozen Windmill supporters managed to raise. So astounding was this cheer, coming from so few throats, that many of the Cliff girls almost lost their own voices in astonishment!

Then these historians go on to describe how Betty's goal fired the whole team to doughty deeds. So fierce was their onslaught that panic seized the Cliff players, so that their shots became wild and uncertain, their captain striving in vain to rally them.

However much the stories vary, one and all agree that Betty was the heroine of the tale. The second goal, secured after some clever passing between the forwards as they swept down the field, also came from Betty's stick.

Once more Miss Battle and her little group were called upon to raise a cheer, and nobly they answered the call.

But it is when they are describing the end of the match that the onlookers speak with bated breath. The score was now two all, and they tell of the Cliff team's frantic efforts to pull themselves together and stem the tide which was flowing against them.

The minutes seemed like hours as the two teams fought the most exciting finish ever seen on the college field.

Even though they seemed to have given up

hope of scoring again, Cliff College were determined to defend their goal to the uttermost, and every attempt to break through was stemmed till the very moment when the referee was raising her whistle to her lips, to signal the end of the game.

In that last tense moment Betty dribbled the ball into the striking circle, and with another of her lightning shots she beat the goal-keeper for the third time, and the ball was no sooner in the net than the whistle sounded " finis " to the game.

Bright-eyed and breathless, Betty beamed on her team of muddy, gallant warriors, and Miss Battle, arms waving wildly, fairly ran on to the field to congratulate them.

" Even the ranks of Tuscany can scarce forbear to cheer," quoted Mary Towle, for the Cliff girls were generously saluting the victors.

It was perhaps the happiest moment Betty had known during this term of change and strife. The long chain of defeat had been broken, and victory had come to Windmill at last!

" It was an epic!" Miss Battle boomed (that is really the only word to describe her most trumpet-like tones!). " An epic game, girls!"

There were hand-shakings and back-slappings,

breathless cheers and happy laughter, as they all strolled off the field and made their way to the changing-rooms.

" If only Prissy had been here!" was the thought that came to Betty's mind. " She always used to come and watch the Windmill-Cliff match."

The college provided an excellent tea, and what a jolly little meal it was, everyone tired and hungry and happy, and eager to discuss every incident of the match!

" After the game's fitful fever, we eat well!" murmured Mary Towle, her mild eyes gleaming as she eyed a very delicious-looking jam roll.

" Is that a quotation, Owl?" drawled Esme. " I seem to have heard something like it before."

But Mary only smiled, munching steadily, and then turned a sympathetic ear to Sonia, who had suddenly remembered an anecdote touching on the family history of the Starforths.

Then came a rush for the train back to Windmill, all looking forward to breaking the news to the stay-at-homes at school.

Miss Battle was as thrilled as any of them,

and no sooner were they in school again than she button-holed Betty, urging her along the corridor towards the junior play-room.

" We'll tell the juniors ourselves, Betty," she beamed. " Come along! I am quite sure they are all dying to know the result, and they shall have it first-hand!"

There was no denying Miss Battle's enthusiasm, and a few moments later she opened the play-room door with a flourish and strode across the threshold, her hand on Betty's shoulder.

" Girls! I've got great news—great news!" she announced, smiling round on the score or so of juniors who had turned in surprise at their entrance. " For the first time in history we have beaten Cliff College on their own ground by three goals to two, and I want to introduce you to the heroine of the match. Betty Lyndon, girls! Betty scored all three goals, and I'm sure Miss Shephard won't mind if we make a little noise now, for I'm going to ask you to give three cheers for Betty. Now, girls—hip, hip, hip——"

Red in the face, the games mistress raised her hand to conduct the rousing cheers which she expected would follow, but not a sound left the juniors' throats.   There was a chill and uncomfortable silence, with a faint shuffle of feet here and there, while many of the juniors seemed to be looking at Madge and Maureen, as if for guidance.

The Terrible Twins, with stony faces, were gazing steadily at the floor.

" Didn't you hear me, children?" Miss Battle brought out at last. " I asked you to——"

" Oh, please don't bother them, Miss Battle," exclaimed Betty, suddenly finding her tongue. " I'm sure they're as pleased about it as we are, really!"

The words came from Betty's lips, though she hardly realized what she was saying. That chill silence had struck her like a slap in the face, and unable to stand there any longer, she turned and hurried out of the room.

It had not been so long since Betty was the most welcome visitor to the juniors' domain, greeted always by the adoring gaze of Madge and Maureen. What had happened to cause this nightmare-like change? Why had they hurt her, humiliated her, in front of Miss Battle? Of course, they were only children and perhaps did not understand, but there must be some reason for it!

Into Betty's mind slipped an echo of a drawling voice:

" Aha! I expect she is winning some more of the juniors over to her side!"

It was of Hilary that Esme had spoken in the train. Was this Hilary's doing? Had she poisoned the juniors' minds in some way? Her cheeks still tingling as if from an unfriendly blow, Betty asked herself these questions again and again, and it seemed to her that all her troubles were due to Hilary and the new head. Nothing had been the same at Windmill since they arrived—everything had gone wrong!

Her mind in a whirl, Betty paused by an open door, for to her ears floated the clear, cool voice of the very girl she was thinking about.

" Yes, this ought to make a jolly good common-room for us seniors, Auntie."

Miss Shephard's voice replied:

" So I think, Hilary. We will get the seniors to move their belongings some time next week, and then the old windmill room will be ready for the builders."

So they were in there, the two of them, plotting and planning! They meant to carry out their threat of doing away with the old windmill common-room, where Prissy's portrait hung, and where she had so often, in those gentle tones of hers, spoken to the girls about history and life.

Betty was almost on the point of rushing in to denounce the head and Hilary there and then, but she stopped herself in time, and unwilling to play the part of an eavesdropper, she went on her way.

One thing was quite clear. The time had come for Betty to gather her forces and strike a blow against the vandals who would spoil Windmill. After resigning their prefectships they had been content just to drift along, but now the time had come to show Miss Shephard what they stood for, and what they felt.

" I'll call another meeting," Betty thought. " I'll make the girls see that they must *act*!"

Meanwhile, in the play-room, Miss Battle had been speaking in her most crushing tones, and the juniors wilted before her icy gaze.

" I don't pretend to understand your conduct," she had told them. " I can't bring myself to speak to you now on such subjects as loyalty to your school and your team and your hockey captain. I can only say that I am shocked—inexpressibly shocked."

So saying, Miss Battle strode from the room, closing the door behind her with no uncertain touch.

The juniors gazed at one another, and Madge drew a deep breath.

"Well, we had to do it, hadn't we?" she appealed to them. "We all agreed to send Betty to Coventry, because Maureen and I found out she had done something really unsporting and rotten. And if you've sent someone to Coventry, you can't give three cheers for them, can you?"

The juniors shook their heads, and for a few moments no one spoke, till the silence was broken from an unexpected quarter.

Isabel Bayley—that queer child—suddenly burst into tears.

CHAPTER VIII

Miss Shephard Wins a Recruit

Seated on her little folding stool, with a large sketch-block on the easel in front of her, Esme Randall was hard at work in a quiet corner of the fields.

She was making a drawing of a little clump of silver birches, with billowy clouds sailing across the sky behind them. The breeze was stirring their slender branches, and slowly the leaves drifted down. "Like gipsy girls losing their finery," thought Esme, and tried to express something of the sadness of autumn in her sketch. There was a gate in the hedge close by, and beyond this a lane down which carts and an occasional car passed now and then, unheeded by the intent young artist.

Though the girls found Esme a trifle affected and "high-brow", there was no doubt she was utterly sincere in her liking for art, and almost all her spare time was spent in making drawings or paintings, many of which were torn up in despair by Esme, who was very critical of her own work.

Esme had drawing lessons at school, but her parents were not very well off, and could not afford special teaching for her. Her great fear was that she would be forced to take a job of some kind when she left school, and never be more than a spare-time artist.

As her pencil busied itself on the paper, Esme was dreaming.

How grand it would be to go to Paris and study in the art schools there, amongst young people all as keenly interested in art as she was herself! She could not imagine a greater happiness, but she was not sure that it would ever be hers.

" You need money for that," she told herself. " And to win scholarships you want lots of talent, and I'm not really certain whether I've got much talent at all. Sometimes I think I have, and sometimes I'm sure I haven't!"

Suddenly Esme was startled out of her dreaming in a very alarming way.

There was the sound of an approaching car, a wild shout, and a tremendous shattering sound that made Esme jump to her feet. A car had come along the lane at a good pace, but instead of rounding the bend it had hurtled on to the grassy verge and hit the gate almost head-on, smashing it into fragments which were tossed on either side like match-sticks. Now, with a shrill grinding of brakes, it was bearing down on Esme, who had been seated close to the gate.

Even in that moment of unexpected peril, Esme did not forget her picture, and she grabbed it and then made a wild leap to one side, just as the car hit the easel. Esme caught her foot on a tussock and fell headlong, while the car slithered to a standstill some yards farther on.

The car was an open tourer, and as she raised herself on one elbow, Esme saw a tall woman stand up beside the driver and turn towards her. It was Miss Audrey Shephard!

The head mistress was quick to recognize Esme, and she jumped out of the car and ran anxiously towards her.

" My dear girl! Are you hurt?"

Esme scrambled to her feet.

" Not a bit, thank you, Miss Shephard."

The driver had jumped down too, and Esme's observant eye noted that he was tall and grey-haired, with a fine dark face that reminded her of Miss Shephard's. At first glance there was something queerly familiar about the driver of the car, and Esme had a feeling she had seen him before somewhere.

"By Jove, I am most tremendously sorry, young lady!" he exclaimed. "Thank heaven you got out of the way in time. The steering jammed as we were coming round the bend, and there was nothing for it but to hit the gate."

"Perhaps this will persuade you that you really do need a new car, John!" said the head, with her quick brilliant smile. "This gentleman is my brother, Esme—John Shephard."

Esme's heart gave a quick jump, for she had discovered why the stranger had seemed so familiar to her. Surely he must be John Shephard, the famous artist! Esme had several prints of his pictures, and many a time she had seen his photo in the papers, though up till now she had never connected him with the new head of Windmill.

"Why, you must be *the* John Shephard!" she could not help bursting out, her eyes shining.

"There may be other John Shephards, for aught I know," he smiled. "But I expect I am the one you mean—the artist. And I do believe I have upset a fellow-artist, for there lies a smashed easel on the grass. Of course you will allow me to replace it."

" Oh, it's only an old one—it really doesn't matter at all," replied Esme.

To think that the wonderful John Shephard was the head's brother! It was the first time Esme had been in the presence of a really great artist, and there was such awe and admiration in the gaze she turned upon him that John Shephard smiled again.

" I see your first thought, like a true artist, was to save your picture," he said. " May I see the sketch?"

He held out his hand—a real artist's hand, Esme noted, with thick capable fingers. Without a word Esme handed him the sketch, and she felt herself trembling while he studied it in silence.

She knew that a man like John Shephard would be incapable of false flattery where art was concerned, and that she might expect his honest opinion, whether for good or bad. Suppose he said she had no talent! Esme felt that the very crisis of her life was at hand.

At length, after what seemed an age, the artist looked up.

" You've a lot to learn, young lady," he said.
" That's true of all of us, for we're all learn-
ing right up to the end. But I think there
is promise here, distinct promise, though, of
course, I couldn't say till I have seen more of
your work. Would that be possible, Audrey?"
he added, turning to the head. " I really feel
I would like to see more of this young artist's
drawings."

Those few words of praise were enough to
set Esme's head in a whirl of happiness. " Promise, distinct promise "—they rang over and
over again like a peal of bells in her mind.

" I'm sure Esme would appreciate your
criticism when you visit the school, John,"
Miss Shephard was saying. " I will take you
along to her study, and you shall both spend
an hour talking about art."

" Then that's settled!" laughed the artist.
" Now I've got to get busy. First I must see
the farmer who owns that gate, and compen-
sate him for smashing it, and then I must get
in touch with a garage and have the car towed
away for repairs. I'm afraid you will have to
walk back to school, Audrey."

" Esme and I will go together," replied the
head. " And do let me implore you, John, not

to have that car patched up any more, but to sell it as scrap-iron, and buy something that can be trusted not to behave so perilously."

Laughing, John Shephard strode away, and Esme found herself taking the footpath back towards school, with the head striding beside her.

" I'm glad my brother took an interest in your work, Esme," said Miss Shephard. " He would not have wanted to see more of it if he had not thought you had some real talent."

Esme sighed rapturously.

" It's heavenly, Miss Shephard!" she exclaimed. " It's like one of my dreams come true!"

Esme had never actively disliked the new head, but now she felt as if she really loved her! The mere fact that Miss Shephard had a brother who was a famous artist was enough to raise her on a pinnacle, where Esme was concerned. As they walked along Esme was filled with a desire to show her gratitude to Miss Shephard for being so helpful and sympathetic.

There was only one thing she could do, and as they turned into the lane that led to the school gates, Esme decided to do it.

" Miss Shephard," she began. " About the

prefectships. I believe you said we would be free to withdraw our resignations, if we thought better of it."

" Indeed I did," replied the head. " Though of course we cannot continue very much longer as we are at present. If you old prefects do not wish to take up your duties again, I shall have to find some other seniors who are willing to do so, though I have purposely delayed it as long as I could."

Esme took a deep breath.

" If you'll let me, Miss Shephard, I should like to take up my prefectship again," she said.

With a little smile, the head glanced at Esme's flushed and excited face.

" I am glad to hear it," she answered. " But are you quite sure you are not doing this, Esme, just because you have found out that my brother is a well-known artist?"

Esme flushed a little more deeply.

" No, Miss Shephard—really I'm not," she protested. " I don't think I was ever very keen on our—our rebellion, only I was carried away by what some of the other girls said. In their hearts I think most of the girls feel the same as I do now, but Bet— but one or two of them are still anxious to carry on."

"Very well," said Miss Shephard. "From this moment you can consider yourself a prefect once more, Esme, and I am sure Hilary will be glad. Try to bring the others to your way of thinking, my dear."

They had reached the school grounds now, and with a brisk step and a nod to Esme, the head passed through the gate leading into her private garden, leaving the newly appointed prefect to wend her way towards the main entrance.

Not that Esme was thinking very much about her prefect's duties. She was wondering when John Shephard would visit the school, and what he would think of her work, and how delightful it would be to spend an hour listening to his criticisms and his talk about pictures. Esme had a hundred problems and difficulties on which she was longing to ask his advice.

These happy dreams were shattered by someone who came racing over the cobbled courtyard and caught Esme by the arm.

"Aren't you coming to the meeting, Esme? It has started already, you know. We must hurry!"

It was Hilda Field, and Esme stared at her rather crossly.

"What on earth are you talking about?" she demanded. "What meeting?"

"Didn't you know Betty had called another meeting of the seniors?" panted Hilda. "Oh, do come along, Esme—don't stand there looking so superior. The head means to turn us out of the windmill common-room next week, and Betty wants us to make a stand against it."

Esme shrugged her shoulders.

"I see," she replied. "Very well, I'll come."

Leaving the impatient Hilda to race ahead, Esme strolled towards the common-room, still carrying her sketching materials. As she entered the room, Betty was making one of her urgent appeals to the girls, who were sitting on the lockers or perched on the table.

". . . and if we don't act now, we may never get a better chance," Betty was saying. "So far we've all stood together, and Miss Shephard hasn't succeeded in getting a single prefect to act for her, except Hilary. But that's not enough, and now we've got another chance to stand up for what we believe to be right."

It was hard to resist Betty when she was in this eloquent mood. Her brown eyes shone as she gazed around at her friends, and she tossed

back her tumbled hair, almost like a war-horse
tossing its mane before going into battle. If
the enthusiasm of the seniors had been dying
down, Betty's words were beginning to kindle
it afresh.

" You've all seen the notice on the board,"
she went on. " Next week Miss Shephard
wants us to move our belongings out of this
common-room, and then the builders will
come along and start turning it into a beastly
lab. Haven't you heard Prissy telling us over
and over again that this old windmill common-
room is a wonderful link with the past, and
that lots of the traditions of the school cluster
around it? There's Prissy's portrait hanging
on the wall, looking down on us, and don't
let's disgrace it, girls."

Betty paused for breath, and Mary Towle
asked : " What do you suggest we should do,
Betty?"

For answer, Betty held up a key.

" That's the key to my locker," she said.
" And each one of you has got a key too. I
suggest we put all our belongings in our lockers,
and then lock them and throw the keys away.
If Miss Shephard wants to turn us out, she will
have to break open the lockers to get at our

things, and that ought to show her how deeply we feel about it."

It was a daring plan, but Betty had no doubt she would be able to carry the girls with her.

"Don't you feel that is the best plan?" she demanded. "Don't you agree with me?"

There was a moment's silence, and then Esme's drawling voice was heard. The young artist was sitting on the edge of the table, swinging a graceful leg.

"I'm afraid I can't agree," she said.

Betty turned towards her in surprise.

"Why not?" she asked sharply.

Like the dropping of a thunderbolt came Esme's reply.

"I've just told Miss Shephard I am willing to become a prefect again. In fact, I am a prefect at this moment, so of course I can't agree to your plan, Betty. And what's more, I don't think any of the others want to do it, only they haven't got the courage to say so!"

CHAPTER IX

Defeat for Betty

Betty took a few quick steps towards the lazy-eyed girl who was sitting so carelessly on the table's edge, swinging her legs and smiling.

"You mean you've let us all down?" Betty burst out. "You've withdrawn your resignation?"

Esme nodded.

"I think it's rather futile to go on with this rebellion business," she drawled. "Miss Shephard is a very fine person, in my opinion. Of course, she different from Prissy, and she's bound to make changes, but—oh, girls, I've had such an adventure this afternoon!"

Esme's thoughts were still full of her meeting with John Shephard, which was so much more important to her than these schoolgirl affairs.

"I nearly got knocked down by a car while I was sketching," she went on, eager to talk about what was uppermost in her mind. "And

who do you think were in the car? Miss Shephard and her brother, and he's none other than
John Shephard, the famous artist, and he looked
at my sketch and said it showed distinct promise, and when he comes to the school he is
going to look at all my pictures, and criticize
them for me. Isn't it great?"

It might seem " great " to Esme, but Betty's
lips curled in contempt as she listened.

" So that's it!" she cried hotly. " I think
it's mean of you, Esme—a downright shame!
Just because they flattered you over some daubs
of paint!"

It was not often that Esme was roused out of
her superior calm, but she took fire now.

" Daubs of paint, indeed!" she exclaimed.
" Don't make yourself ridiculous, Betty, by
talking of what you know nothing whatever
about. Pictures are far more important than
hockey or silly little schemes for throwing
locker keys away!"

" And you seem to think they're more important than being loyal to your chums and to
what you agreed to do!" Betty retorted.

" Hear, hear!" chimed in Sonia. " 'Be loyal
unto death!' That was on the crest of one of
the Starforth knights who——"

" Oh, stop it, Sonia, for goodness sake!" Esme interrupted. " I'm not in the mood to listen to family histories now. Look here, girls, don't you see how senseless it is to go against Miss Shephard like this? She is bound to have her way in the end. After all, I think there is a good deal in her point of view. She just wants to make Windmill a bit more modern and up-to-date."

" She certainly seems to know how to win you over!" said Betty. " But just because she has turned your head by praising your pictures, it doesn't mean that the rest of us are going to change our minds or our plans. We can still be loyal to Prissy just the same, and as prefects weren't invited to this meeting, I think it was pretty low-down of you to come and listen."

But Esme stood her ground.

" You talk a lot about Prissy," she said, with a laugh. " But do you really think Miss Jennings cares so much about what happens here now? Why, I don't believe she has written to you once since term began, and we all know what a favourite of hers you used to be!"

What a cruel knack Esme had of aiming at her opponent's weak spot, and probing the wound! Betty dropped her eyes for a moment,

afraid lest the girls might see she had been
hurt, but a moment later she raised them again.

" It doesn't matter whether Prissy has written
or not," she replied. " Even if I never heard
from her again, I should still think she is one
of the most wonderful people in the world."

Esme smiled.

" I ought to warn you that you are making
yourself unpopular amongst the juniors, old
thing," she said. " What is this story I hear
about them refusing to cheer the conquering
heroine when she came back from the Cliff
College match?"

Some of the senior girls began to look rather
uneasy at this. They, too, had heard rumours
that Betty's one-time popularity amongst the
juniors had waned, if not vanished away. Of
course, no one bothered about the youngsters
really, but still it was not nice to feel you ran
the risk of unpopularity if you followed Betty.

Did Betty feel that the tide was beginning
to flow against her? At any rate, she made a
bold attempt to remove the chief cause of the
trouble.

" As this is a meeting for non-prefects, I vote
we ask Esme to leave," she said.

Sonia popped up from her seat, mindful of

the many insults Esme had hurled against the Starforths.

" I second that!" she cried.

But at once Gladys Sims, who was one of Esme's admirers, moved that she be allowed to remain, and this was seconded by Gladys's friend, Joan. The meeting was facing a deadlock!

" Put it to the vote," suggested Mary Towle, her eyes blinking wisely behind the large spectacles.

They voted by a show of hands, and out of the thirty girls present, nineteen voted that Esme should be allowed to remain, with eleven against it. A victory for Esme, and she was quick to seize her advantage.

" Thanks!" she drawled. " And since I am graciously permitted to remain, I should like to make a suggestion. Why not vote on this plan of Betty's about the locker keys? Not by putting up hands, because some of you might be scared of Betty's wrath if you voted against it. Have a proper secret ballot, on slips of paper."

" What do you think, Betty?" asked Hilda.

Betty shrugged her shoulders. Her impetuous nature had little sympathy for the methods of the ballot-box and voting-slip. She had hoped to rouse them all to general enthusiasm, and to be well on the way to having the whole plan cut-and-dried by now. If only that supercilious Esme had not turned up to spoil it all!

" It seems a waste of time to me," she said. " We all seemed to be agreed before Esme came in. But do as you like."

Mary and Sonia busied themselves preparing the slips. Thirty were needed—for Esme, as a prefect, was not voting—and these were handed round to the girls.

" Put ' yes ' if you agree to Betty's plan, and ' no ' if you don't," Mary said.

Heads were bent over the slips, and pencils wrote the fatal words. Someone brought out a very stained beret, and this was used for collecting the papers, all of them folded to conceal the word. Mary was acting as vote-counter, and they watched her painstakingly divide the slips into two heaps at the end of the table. They could see that one heap was much bigger than the others, though they did not yet know which was the " Ayes " and which the " Noes ".

Mary's face was looking very solemn as she completed the counting.

"Do hurry up, Mary!" cried Betty impatiently, a dreadful doubt beginning to seize her. "Surely you have had time to count them by now. What is the result?"

Mary cleared her throat, seeming to find some difficulty in speaking.

"I'm awfully sorry, Betty," she said. "But it's twenty-three against, and only seven in favour of the plan."

Poor Betty! She had thought that Esme might find one or two supporters, but she had never dreamed it would be as bad as this. How could she help feeling bitterly humiliated? And this was not the only blow she had received just lately, for the strange conduct of the juniors had hurt her far more than she would confess, and now it seemed they were all deserting her, even her own class-mates and companions were growing tired of the fight for Windmill's traditions and Prissy's memory! Only six girls beside herself had been in favour of the bold plan that might have brought Miss Shephard to her senses.

It was one of Betty's rules, however, always to take a defeat with a good grace.

"So that's that!" she said, trying to speak lightly. "Will those six who voted in favour come to my study this evening, because I think we will still make our protest, even though there are so few of us."

She found it hard to speak steadily, and turned to stare out of a window to hide her trembling lips. Yes, it had been a hard blow, but she was vowing that it should not mean the end of the rebellion. She would still fight on, whatever happened! But how different this was from that first meeting at the beginning of the term, when the standard of revolt had been raised, and they had all seemed to be on her side! What a difference a few short weeks could make!

There was a good deal of uncomfortable shuffling of feet and coughing amongst the girls, for no one quite knew what to say, and everyone was glad when the tea-bell was heard.

" Thank goodness!" exclaimed Hilda. " I'm as hungry as a hunter."

The room quickly emptied, and strange to say it was Esme who lingered behind, glancing towards Betty, who still stood gazing out of the window. A pang of sympathy seized Esme; she felt so happy herself, it seemed a pity that Betty couldn't be happy too.

She strolled along and gently touched Betty's arm.

" I say, don't take it to heart, old thing," she said.

There was no reply from Betty.

" Of course, although I'm a prefect again now, I shan't breathe a word about your plan," went on Esme. " You didn't know I was a prefect when I came in, so it's all in confidence, as far as I'm concerned."

Still no answer from that brown-haired girl gazing so stonily out of the window, and giving up her attempt at sympathy, Esme drifted gracefully away, humming a tune under her breath.

CHAPTER X

Highwayman's Cliff

For the first time in her school life Betty Lyndon was missing hockey practice for no reason at all, or, at least, for no reason that could be explained to Miss Battle, that stern enemy of all slackers and shirkers. The truth was, Betty wanted to get right away from school for a little while, to collect her thoughts and try to see things more clearly.

Her steps had turned instinctively towards Beacon Hill, and she was climbing the steep path that led up to the old tower perched right at the top, against the autumn sky. She would make her way up the crumbling stone stairway, and from that look-out post she would be able to gaze across country to the little white house where Prissy had gone to live.

Even though she seemed so cut off from her adored old friend, Betty felt that it would comfort her to look across the space that separated them, and perhaps in some mysterious manner

Prissy's wisdom would wing its way across the miles, and give Betty the help and the strength that she felt she needed.

" If only I could make the girls feel as I feel!" thought Betty, picking her way between yellow-starred gorse, higher and higher. " But they're all getting tired of the rebellion, and everyone seems to be turning against me. Even Sonia and Mary and the others who voted for my plan the other day are not really keen on it in their hearts."

It was a strange sensation for the once-popular Betty to feel that she stood alone in the school; yet that was how she had come to feel, more and more as the days went by. Perhaps the attitude of the juniors hurt most of all, though, of course, Betty would not confess that she cared a little bit for what they did or said; yet she shrank inwardly when that stony look came over the faces of Madge and Maureen whenever they caught sight of her or she had occasion to speak to them. It was all so stupid, so inexplicable, so unfair!

" What have I done?" Betty asked herself fiercely. " I've only tried to be loyal to Prissy and the good old ways of Windmill. When this term began it was Hilary who stood alone,

and now it's me. Well, I won't give up, whatever happens!"

What a blow the result of that voting had
been! Only six of them on her side! Betty was
doubtful whether it would be wise for just
those few to carry out her idea about the
common-room lockers. Would it not be more
like a confession of weakness, when there were
so many who had not agreed to the plan? Yet
she could not bear to do nothing at all, when
these vandals were striking a blow at the very
heart of Windmill School.

Oh, how muddled and difficult everything
was! What would Prissy say? Would she
approve or condemn? Betty could not tell,
and in her present troubled mood she told herself that she might never hear from Prissy
again or look into those wise and gentle eyes.

Tossing the brown hair back from her forehead, Betty stopped short to get her breath,
and it was then that she heard a faint whining
sound that seemed to come from her left,
beyond a clump of bushes. Curious, she moved
in that direction.

" I'm quite near Highwayman's Cliff," she
thought.

On one side of Beacon Hill was a sheer cliff,

just as if someone had cut it with a gigantic knife, as one cuts a slice of cake. It had its name from an old story of a highwayman who, pursued by enemies, had jumped his horse from the cliff-top and crashed to destruction far below.

Perhaps there was no truth in the old story, though Sonia would maintain that one of her ancestors had been foremost in the pursuit, and had actually been near enough to see that terrible leap, and had described it all in a letter to one of his Starforth relatives a hundred and fifty years ago!

Pushing her way through the bushes, Betty came to the edge of Highwayman's Cliff, and going down on hands and knees she peered cautiously over.

" Oh, the poor little thing!" she exclaimed.

A mongrel puppy had fallen on to a narrow ledge about ten feet down, and it was from his shaggy little throat that the unhappy whining sounds came. He was making clumsy efforts to climb up again, and every moment Betty feared he would loose his footing and go hurtling down to the valley beneath.

" Keep still, old fellow—keep still!" she called, but her voice only had the effect of making the puppy more excited, and with yelping barks he redoubled his efforts to climb up.

Betty's quick brown eyes were measuring the slope just beneath her. As far as the ledge it was not quite sheer, and she noted certain footholds and handholds that would help a climber. It would be risky, but as long as she kept her head, she felt sure she could clamber down to the ledge and save the little shaggy creature from falling.

Whether she would be able to climb up again with the puppy was another matter, but there was no time to consider that now, and with lips set rather grimly, Betty lowered herself over the edge.

After all the worry and self-questioning and mental strain she had been through lately, it was a relief to have something definite to do, even though it was such a risky act as climbing down Highwayman's Cliff to rescue a puppy.

" I mustn't think of the drop," she whispered. " I've just got to work my way down, foot by foot."

Clinging to tufts of grass, finding perilous footholds in cracks and crevices, the rebel schoolgirl clambered down that perilous slope. She came of a long line of soldiers who had served their country in India, and a call for plucky action would never find Betty hanging back.

Beneath her she could hear the puppy's eager yelps; she dared not look down, but as long as she could hear the puppy, she knew that he was still on the ledge and that there was still a chance of rescuing him.

Surely she must be near the ledge now! It had not looked so very far from above, but now she was climbing down it seemed as if the slope would never end. A tuft of grass came away suddenly from the crumbling soil, and she slithered wildly for several feet, her heart beating fast, telling herself that she was sliding to her doom.

And then something touched her foot, and she ventured to look down, and saw that it was the puppy, reared on his hind legs, eager to welcome his gallant young rescuer. Next moment her feet were on the ledge, and she bent down and picked up the whimpering, shaggy little creature, hugging him close to her, his warm red tongue licking her neck. As she did so, Betty caught one glimpse of the abyss yawning below, and she jerked her head up quickly, trying to forget it.

" We've got to get up again, doggie!" she said, a little shakily. " Or shall we just stay down here and shout for help?"

No, she would have to attempt the climb, Betty felt. Beacon Hill was a lonely spot, and it might be hours—days, perhaps—before anyone sighted them on the ledge.

" But how am I going to carry you, old chap?" she said, gazing at the puppy.

Not that the puppy was worrying about the problem. With the instinct of his kind, he felt that he had found a faithful friend, and that all his troubles were over!

Betty remembered suddenly that she had a leather belt coiled in the pocket of her blazer. She took it out and buckled it around her outside the blazer, so that she could put the puppy inside it and button him up, with no danger of his slipping down.

" Keep still in there, boy," she warned him. " We've got to climb up, and the sooner the better."

Choosing her first foothold with the utmost care, Betty started the climb, knowing that going up would be much more difficult than coming down, especially as there was always the fear that the puppy might wriggle out of her blazer. She prayed that the little creature might have enough sense to keep still.

Had the top of the cliff receded in some magic way? It certainly seemed so to the girl who lay full length on the grassy slope, working her way up, little by little.

She was half-way up when a knob of earth on which her right foot was resting gave way altogether, and her feet seemed to be swinging in mid-air. She was holding on only by her outstretched hands, and sudden panic took possession of her, in spite of herself. She felt she could neither go on nor go back, and to make matters worse, the puppy began to scramble about inside her blazer, and if he fell out she knew she could do nothing to save him.

Her voice was raised in a despairing cry.

" Help! Help!"

Something made her look down over her shoulder for a moment, and she saw with a shudder that she had been unintentionally working her way sideways as well as upwards, so that she was no longer over the ledge. Once she started slipping there was nothing between her and the sheer, deadly drop.

" Help! Oh, please help!"

The cry echoed away, and it was heard by a grizzled, grey-haired man who had been searching for something a little way round the shoulder of the hill. With a start of surprise, he began to run towards the cliff edge.

" 'Tis a lassie's voice," he murmured. " And it comes frae the cliff. What in heaven's name is amiss?"

It was Andrew McTavish, the gardener of Windmill School, who had heard the despairing call, and his weather-beaten face wrinkled in horror as he peered over the brink and saw the girl clinging to the slope.

" Keep your heart up, lassie, and dinna let go!" he burst out, and then, as Betty raised her head to look upwards at the sound of his voice: " Wisht! 'Tis Miss Betty! Bide there a wee while, and I'll ha' ye up, safe and sound!"

In his younger days Andrew had been a shepherd in the Highlands, and not seldom had he climbed down some dangerous cliff to rescue a lost lamb. Now, though his limbs were stiffer than of old, he was quick to clamber to Betty's help, and oh, what blessed relief she felt when Andrew's strong arm was round her.

" There now, we'll get up together in graun' style," Andrew panted, and then for the first time caught a glimpse of the puppy peeping from Betty's blazer. " Heavens alive! So ye've got the doggie there. I was hunting for the wee rascal when I heard your call."

" He fell on the ledge," Betty panted, as with Andrew's help she recommenced her climb. " I never dreamt he was yours, Andrew, but I'm so glad he's safe. I heard him whimpering down there, and I was trying to rescue him. I never knew you had a dog, Andrew."

The old gardener hesitated, as he helped Betty over a difficult patch.

" Weel now, in a manner o' speaking, he's not my own," he replied. " But I was in a rare state aboot him all the same, for 'twould have broken his mistress's heart if she'd lost the pup, and I'm thinking she'll be verra grateful to you, Miss Betty, when I tell her how ye rescued him."

They were scrambling over the edge now, and with a sigh of relief Betty sank down on the ground, keeping tight hold of the puppy. Old Andrew stood looking down at her.

" Ay, ye were always a brave lassie," he said. " There's not many would have risked so much for a wee dog."

" I'm afraid I wasn't brave enough," Betty

laughed, smoothing the hair away from her forehead. " I was in a terrible funk when you heard me calling, Andrew. Thanks ever so much for saving me and the puppy. What's his name?"

" Bingo," said Andrew.

" And who does he belong to?" Betty asked.

The old gardener shook his head.

" In a manner o' speaking, that's a kind of secret," he answered. " I canna tell ye, Miss Betty, for I'm under a vow o' secrecy. But what aboot yoursel', now? What are ye doing up on Beacon Hill, when all the lassies are at their hockey, and ye the captain o' the whole game?"

Betty turned her head to where the top of Beacon Tower could be seen above a tangle of trees and bushes.

" I'm going to climb to the top of the tower," she said. "I say, Andrew, you haven't forgotten Miss Jennings yet, have you?"

" Forgotten her?" cried Andrew. " I would be forgetting my own name first, Miss Betty. For ten years I worked for her, and a sweeter lady never breathed in the land!"

Betty smiled. It was always so nice to hear Prissy praised.

" She is sweet, isn't she, Andrew? Well, from the top of Beacon Tower you can just catch a glimpse of the little white house where she's living now. That's why I like to climb up there, and I'd love to do it one night," she added, half to herself, " and see Prissy's lighted window twinkling away through the dark!"

There was an odd look in the old gardener's eyes as he looked down at Betty. She had always been one of his favourites.

" Weel, I'll no' be hindering ye," he said, as Betty jumped to her feet. " But I'd take care when climbing those old steps in the tower, Miss Betty, for they're none too safe. And now gie me that wee rascal of a puppy, and I'll see he doesna fall over the cliff again. 'Tis time I was turning back, ye ken."

So they parted, Betty gaily waving her hand as she hurried off towards the tower, while old Andrew began to plod downhill with the puppy who had been the cause of that exciting adventure.

There was little that went on in Windmill School that the old gardener did not know about, and he was well aware that this term was not proving a very happy one for Betty. His eyes, under the grizzled brows, were just a little dim as he tramped on his way.

" So she climbs up tae the tower-top, just to see the white house beyond the hill," he murmured. " I'm thinking she's lonesome, in spite o' all her merry smiles—puir wee motherless bairn!"

CHAPTER XI

"Many Happy Returns!"

In the little garden at the back of Andrew's cottage, Isabel Bayley stooped to hug the shaggy, quivering form of Bingo, who had reared up with his paws on her shoulders and was trying to lick her face with a warm red tongue.

" Ay, there's nae doot he's mighty fond o' ye, missy," smiled the old gardener.

" And I'm mighty fond of him too," murmured Isabel. " I love William of Orange ever so much, but I love Bingo ten times more, don't I, Bingo, darling?"

Let it be admitted, here and now, that Bingo was Isabel's secret. It was now more than a fortnight since she had first set eyes on the mongrel puppy, on one of her solitary walks, when she had heard him whining unhappily amongst a group of rough, teasing boys.

Those who knew Isabel only as a queer, shy child would have been amazed at the pluck with which she darted into the midst of Bingo's tormentors, snatched him up and, with flashing eyes, dared the lads to lay another finger on him.

The boys had been quelled, put to flight, by something that shone out of Isabel's eyes like a flare of anger and contempt, and she had walked away, hugging the puppy, who from that moment became her adoring slave.

Thereafter Isabel had to grapple with the knottiest problem she had ever faced in her young life. What was she to do with the trusting, shaggy little creature who snuggled up against her, as if crying out for protection and love? Was she to turn him on to the roads again, to face the miserable life of a homeless stray, and perhaps to be taken up by the police and sent away to be " put to sleep " because no one would own him? Isabel's whole being revolted at the very thought of it!

But the girls of Windmill School were not allowed to keep dogs, and Isabel had terrifying visions of Bingo being snatched from her arms by a mistress—perhaps by Miss Shephard herself—and consigned to outer darkness.

In her doubt and perplexity she had met Andrew, and the kindly old gardener had offered to keep Bingo for her till the end of the term, and to let her see him whenever she wished, and perhaps take him for walks, if it could be managed secretly. Isabel had insisted that the whole plan should be kept as secret as possible, for she was still haunted by fears that she might lose her shaggy pet.

That was why Isabel had developed the puzzling habit of slipping away from the other girls, and always looking as if she was hiding some guilty secret.

She had been waiting in the little garden when Andrew returned from his ramble with the puppy, and Bingo had flown to her arms with little, happy whimperings.

" I'm glad tae have brought him back safe and sound," Andrew said, tilting back his hat and gazing down at the pair of them. " And since there's nae harm done, I'll tell ye that he had a verra narrow escape, up there on the hill."

Isabel's eyes were raised in anxious query.

" A narrow escape? Oh, Andrew, what do you mean?"

" The wee pup slipped awa' from me, up nigh the crest o' Beacon Hill, amongst the gorse bushes," explained Andrew. " I was mighty bothered aboot it, I can tell ye, when I searched and searched, and never a sign o' Bingo. ' 'Twill break the lassie's heart, if I come back without the puppy,' I said to maself. And then, on a sudden, I heard a cry for help! Forgetting aboot the wee animal for the moment, I scrambled through the bushes, with that cry in my ears, coming from the chasm—the Highwayman's Cliff, ye ken."

With wide-open eyes, Isabel was following this narrative, and even Bingo stopped wriggling, just as if he knew this was the story of his rescue!

" I'm telling ye, my heart nearly jumped into my mouth when I got to the brink o' it," went on the old gardener. " For aboot six feet frae the top, a lassie was clinging. Aye, and she had a Windmill blazer on too, and when she looked up I saw 'twas Betty Lyndon."

" Betty!" breathed Isabel.

" Aye, and when I clambered doon to gie her a hand, I saw something else, for inside her blazer she had the wee dog tucked, all safe and cosy. Och! 'Twas the pluckiest thing I ever saw in my life, for puir wee Bingo had fallen on to the ledge below, and Miss Betty had climbed doon and saved him, and she took a terrible risk to do it, though, thank God, it ended well."

Isabel's face had gone even paler than usual, and her eyes never left Andrew's face. She had such a queer haunted expression, indeed, that the gardener patted her head comfortingly.

" There, there! No need tae tak' it to heart, missy!" he said. " The wee pup's safe as ever he was, and I warrant by this time he's forgotten all aboot the fright he had. And noo I can hear the tea-bell, so ye'd best hurry awa', and I'll gie Master Bingo his minced meat and biscuits. Come awa', ye wee rascal!"

Isabel hid her face in Bingo's thick fur for a moment, then sprang to her feet and ran off as if some enemy were pursuing her, and Andrew shook his head as he watched her, for he could never quite understand this queer child, with her passionate love of animals, her shy ways and strange moods.

Isabel was three minutes late for tea, and received a reproof from Miss Darkin, and perhaps it was this that caused her to lose her appetite. She ate very little of the bread-and-butter, plum cake, and fresh fruit salad that was provided at the juniors' table.

" It's my belief that Isabel is going completely crackers," whispered Madge to Maureen. " I pushed my private pot of strawberry jam across to her, and told her she could take a spoonful, but she didn't seem to see it at all!"

" Fancy not seeing strawberry jam!" Maureen giggled. " I can always see it a mile off!"

However, the Terrible Twins had more important matters to consider. They were a very tenacious pair, once they had decided on some particular line of conduct, and they were still intent on making it quite clear that Betty had been dethroned from their favour and that Hilary had taken her place.

As the leaders in the junior play-room, they carried their schoolmates along with them, and Betty was still in Coventry, as far as the younger girls were concerned.

" It's jolly strange that Betty's and Hilary's birthdays should both come to-morrow," murmured Madge. " It will give us a chance to show that we haven't forgotten that ragged study, and the broken porcelain statue."

" It won't be any use unless we all agree to do it together, though," replied Maureen. " The others will have to be in it too."

Madge nodded.

" Oh, they'll be in it all right," she said confidently. " We'll see to that."

To understand this little conversation, it is necessary to explain a very old custom at Windmill School. Whenever any member of the Sixth Form had a birthday, she was always greeted by a chorus of " Many Happy Returns!" from the juniors when she entered the hall for morning assembly. The juniors made it their business to note the dates of all Sixth Form birthdays for this very purpose. No one knew when or how the custom had originated, but it formed a pleasant little link between the girls at the top of the school and the juniors, and Miss Shephard had seen no reason to interfere with it.

It was this little ceremony that had given the Terrible Twins their new idea, and that evening they expounded it to the other members of the play-room.

The juniors very rarely disagreed with any plan put forward by the twins, and the only note of protest and disagreement came from a very unexpected quarter.

Isabel Bayley had been bending over the little cage where she kept the pet mouse, but on hearing the plan suggested by Madge and

Maureen, she sprang to her feet in dismay.

" Oh, you can't—you can't do that!" she burst out. " It isn't right, I'm sure it isn't!"

" Yes, it is, you poor simp," retorted Madge. " You don't know how unsporting Betty has been to Hilary, but we've had proof that she did something so rotten and mean that she deserves to be paid out. We've all agreed on the plan, and so must you."

Trembling, Isabel stood her ground.

" I shan't! I won't!" she cried.

Quick to resent this rebellion against their authority, the Terrible Twins were already bearing down on the luckless Isabel.

" We'll take William of Orange away from her," murmured Madge. " That will bring her to her senses."

Divining their intention, Isabel snatched up the cage and sprang away, and after a breathless chase she managed to dodge her way to the door, fling it open and retreat wildly up the corridor.

" Oh, let her go," panted Maureen. " She's only bluffing, I think, and anyway, she's quite crackers. We needn't bother about her."

After recovering their breath, the twins seemed to feel that a little more explanation was due to their friends, who had hitherto been kept in ignorance of the awful extent of Betty's wrongdoing. Madge and Maureen always found it hard to keep a secret, and now at last they felt they could not keep it to themselves any longer.

" Perhaps you all ought to know what Betty did," began Madge. " You remember that time when Hilary's study was ragged?"

" Yes, rather!" nodded the juniors.

" We had proof that it was Betty who did it," went on Maureen, taking up the tale. " We found a note with her initials on it, only we didn't show it to Hilary for fear of getting Betty into awful trouble."

" And she smashed a little statue that Hilary was awfully fond of," added Madge. " Hilary cried about it, didn't she, Maureen?"

" Don't talk about it, though," Maureen warned them. " It's still got to be a secret, because if Miss Shephard found out, Betty might be expelled. But now you know why we sent Betty to Coventry, and why we must all carry out our plan to-morrow morning."

There were general cries of agreement at this. Besides, didn't they all know that the seniors themselves were beginning to turn against Betty? Already Esme Randall was established as a prefect again, and only yesterday the news had come that Hilda Field had also withdrawn her resignation and was back in her old place. The tide of events was turning heavily against Betty, and no doubt it would not be long before the other old prefects thought better of it and submitted to the new head.

Perhaps it was just an example of the " herd instinct " that was making the juniors unite against Betty!

However that may be, they were all agog to carry out their plan next morning, and there was a good deal of wriggling and fidgeting as they took their seats in the hall.

It was nearly nine, and Andrew McTavish was ringing the bell in the courtyard, as he had done for so many years past, to call the girls in to morning assembly. After the juniors had taken their places, the seniors began to file in, and at the end of the procession would come the Sixth Form girls, followed by the mistresses.

Hilary was amongst the first to come in, and her arrival was greeted by a lusty shout from young throats: " Many Happy Returns, Hilary!" Her grey eyes smiling, Hilary waved her hand in response.

A moment later Betty entered the hall, and

as she did so, an audible hiss rose from the juniors and died away, broken only by a gasping sound which might or might not have been Isabel Bayley's forlorn attempt to give the birthday greeting.

A tense hush settled over the hall for a moment, and on many junior faces there was a half-frightened look, as if suddenly they realized the enormity of what they had done. All eyes were turned towards Betty, who was making her way steadily to her seat, looking neither to the right nor to the left.

As far as outward appearances went, it was Hilary who showed most signs of confusion. Though she had been singled out for this special act of favouritism, she did not seem to be at all happy about it, for the colour had mounted to her cheeks, usually so cool and pale. She turned round quickly to face Betty, and she caught a look of pain in Betty's brown eyes that sent a pang to her own heart.

So far during this eventful term at Windmill, there had been very little sympathy between Betty and Hilary, one of them representing the old order and the other the new. They had quarrelled, and were generally looked upon as enemies and rivals.

That look of pain in Betty's eyes, caught only for a fleeting moment, was enough to win Hilary's sympathy. She could not guess why the juniors had chosen to be so unthinkingly cruel over this matter of the birthday greetings; whatever the reason, she felt that she must show that she herself was no party to it.

She held out her hand to Betty.

" It's your birthday too, isn't it, Betty?" she said, in a clear voice that was heard throughout the hall. " Many happy returns, dear."

Betty took no notice of the proffered hand. In her present frame of mind it seemed to her that Hilary was publicly showing off her own magnanimity. She did not want Hilary's pity, and would not accept it in front of all those curious, staring eyes.

Already the mistresses were coming in, and the incident was over. The morning hymn was sung, but Betty's usually clear treble was not raised with the other voices, and she stood staring at the printed page in front of her, seeing nothing, hearing nothing except the hiss that had greeted her, rising and falling and dying away.

After prayers, Miss Shephard made an announcement.

" I want the whole school to assemble here immediately after tea this evening," she said. " It is my wish to say a few words to you about what I think should be the new spirit of our school, and also to explain the changes which I know have caused a little doubt in some of your minds."

The head paused, and for an instant her fine black eyes rested on Betty, sitting in her place, her gaze fixed on the floor.

" I am so glad that several of our old prefects are taking up their duties again," went on Miss Shephard. " I am hoping that by this evening they will all have signified their wish to act again. After to-day it will be impossible for me to reinstate any of the old prefects, but I am hoping they will all decide, for the good of the school, to return to their posts of duty. Very well, girls. You may dismiss."

CHAPTER XII

A Birthday Present

Tap, tap!

" Come in!"

A rattling and fumbling at the door handle.

" *Come in!*" called Betty, more loudly.

It was in the half-hour before afternoon school, and Betty was sitting at the little desk in her study, looking over some history, forcing herself to concentrate on the notes she had taken at Miss Darkin's last lecture. She was looking pale and tired, and the hand which turned over the papers trembled a little.

She was having a hard task to prevent anxious nagging thoughts from interrupting her work. Such, for instance, as:

" I'm glad I didn't shake hands with her, considering it must be she who has turned the juniors against me. It *must* be, and yet——"

Betty was of an honest and unsuspicious nature, not given to thinking ill of her fellows, and she was forced to admit that she had no real proof that Hilary had poisoned the minds of the younger girls. Yet if not, why were they behaving so outrageously? She had no doubt that Madge and Maureen were the ringleaders, the twins who had almost worshipped the ground she stood on, only a few short weeks ago.

Even her own class-mates were beginning to look askance at her, she fancied. It was true that loyal chums like Mary Towle and Sonia had gone out of their way to be extra nice to her that morning, but she thought she detected something forced even in their friendliness.

" I expect they'll all swing over to Miss Shephard's side at the meeting to-night," thought Betty, looking up from a note on Cromwell's foreign policy. " And the head will make a speech sneering at Prissy and hinting that she was old-fashioned. . . . Oh, if only Prissy would write! It's getting so hard to stick up for her all alone!"

Whatever was that fumbling and scraping at the door?

" Come in!" cried Betty, for the third time.

The door opened to admit the timid, shrinking form of Isabel Bayley, clasping an object which, to Betty's surprise, turned out to be the cage in which she kept her pet mouse.

" Hullo, Isabel!" said Betty. " What's the matter?"

For one second Isabel looked as if she meant to turn tail and fly away, but then she forced herself to take a few steps forward.

" Oh, it's just—just——" she stammered, and then blurted out: " Many Happy Returns, Betty."

" Thank you," Betty replied, looking at her curiously.

Isabel held the cage containing the white mouse.

" Don't think it's cheek of me, Betty, but I want you to take William of Orange as a—as a birthday present," she said, speaking hurriedly. " You'll love William, he's ever so cute, and if—if you're feeling lonely or—or upset, you don't know what a comfort he is, with his sweet little ways, and it's better to give him brown bread when you feed him, not white, and—oh, please take him!"

Putting aside her notes, Betty rose to her feet. She had become aware that Isabel was on the verge of tears, and she had a dim idea, too, that William of Orange was one of the little girl's most prized possessions.

On a sudden impulse she bent and kissed the woebegone little face in front of her, and somehow it seemed to her that Isabel was not unlike what she herself had been at that age. Only she had had Prissy to turn to—Prissy with her gentle voice and understanding heart. Isabel, it seemed, had only her pets to comfort her, and here she was, offering William of Orange as a birthday present! Was the child trying to make up for the way the juniors had behaved that morning?

" It's ever so nice of you, Isabel," Betty said, smiling down at her. " Only I'm rather afraid William wouldn't be happy away from you. Animals are like that, you know, when they are taken away from someone they're very fond of. It might break his heart."

Isabel's lips trembled.

" Do you—do you really think so?"

" My father had a terrier once," Betty went on. " He lives in India, you know, and once when he came home for eight months' leave, he left the terrier behind him, and it pined away and died. Daddy was awfully upset about it."

" It would be terrible if William were to die," Isabel whispered. " But I so wanted you to have him, Betty."

Betty took the cage and peeped through at William, who was calmly washing his whiskers, quite unaware that his fate was trembling in the balance.

" I'll tell you what we'll do," Betty decided. " I'll take him as a present from you, and you shall look after him for me, for I'm sure you know far more about white mice than I do."

A gust of wind rattled the window-pane, and in the distance thunder rumbled. It looked as if some rough autumn weather was sweeping up from the south-west.

" Perhaps it would be best like that," said Isabel. " William's terribly frightened of storms, and I know how to comfort him, you see, but—but he's got to be *yours*, really."

" Yes, he'll be really mine," agreed Betty.

The child stretched out her hands for the cage, her eyes fixed on Betty's face. Was she noting the haggard look, so unlike the usual healthy glow on Betty's cheeks? Clasping the cage to her dress, she backed slowly towards the door.

" I'll do it!" she then burst out. " I'll tell them! Everything is my fault, and I'm the wickedest girl in the school, only I didn't do it for my own sake. I'll put everything right!"

Another distant rumble of thunder followed this strange outburst, and it was accompanied by the bell ringing for afternoon school. With a gasp, Isabel vanished from Betty's astonished gaze.

CHAPTER XIII

Isabel makes a Confession

While the Third Form were studying *As You Like It* that afternoon, a smudged and ill-spelt note was passed along to Madge.

"*I must see you and Moreen privatly in the lumber room after lessons. Very important and secret. Please be there.—Isabel.*"

Madge handed the note to Maureen, who sat next to her.

"The kid's crazy, I believe," she whispered. "But we'd better see what she wants. Perhaps she wants to say she's sorry for being such a traitor this morning when the rest of us hissed!"

"Perhaps——" began Maureen, but her whispered view of the problem was cut short by Miss Moore, who asked her to repeat the first lines of the speech "All the world's a stage".

It was lucky that Miss Moore did not choose Isabel for recitation that afternoon, for in her present troubled frame of mind William of

Orange's young mistress would certainly not have done justice to the poetry.

As soon as lessons were over, Isabel darted away to the lumber-room, a rather dusty retreat which was often used for secret conclaves. The Terrible Twins found her sitting on an empty trunk, a very tragic expression on her face, but she jumped to her feet when they entered.

" Please shut the door!" she burst out.

" What on earth is tickling you, Isabel?" said Madge, as she closed the door. " If it's about this morning, you needn't worry, though it was mean of you to go against the rest of us. That's what they call being a blackfoot——"

" Blackleg," corrected her twin.

" Well, it's all the same thing," cried Madge. " For goodness sake, don't keep interrupting me, Maureen. It's your worst fault, you know. You just can't let me——"

" Listen!" exclaimed Isabel desperately, anxious to prevent the twins from embarking on one of their squabbles. " I believe I know why you put Betty into Coventry, and why you're so much against her. You think she ragged Hilary's study that time, and broke the little statue."

The twins nodded.

" Well, she didn't!" Isabel brought out. " It was *me*!"

All that afternoon a storm had been circling in the neighbourhood, never quite coming overhead, and again a mutter of thunder was heard in the lumber-room. But if a thunder-bolt had dropped on the school, Madge and Maureen could scarcely have been more startled.

" *What?*" they gasped. " But we found a note, signed with Betty's initials!"

" I wrote it," Isabel confessed. " I know it was the wickedest thing anybody has ever done in Windmill, but I didn't do it for my own sake, it was for Bingo's! And please don't tell about Bingo, or they'll take him away and put him to sleep. Oh, I'm so unhappy!"

Isabel sank down on the trunk and began to sob, and then with an effort pulled herself together, determined to go through with her confession to the bitter end. For once, the twins seemed bereft of speech, and were staring at Isabel as if she was some strange being from another world!

" Bingo's my dog—a stray dog I found," Isabel went on in rather quavery tones. " The gardener is keeping him for me, and I love him better than anything in the world, and I'm so afraid if they find out about him, they'll take him away, and—and one day soon after I'd found him he got away from Andy's cottage, and before I could stop him, he'd run into the school."

Isabel paused for breath, and then, as the spellbound twins seemed waiting to drink in her words, she plunged into her story once again.

" Nobody was about just then, but the door of Hilary's study was a little bit open, and Bingo pushed his way through. He is a regular little mischief, but the darlingest dog all the same, and—oh, it was terrible! He jumped up and knocked the statue over, and the ink too, before I could grab him. I knew if they found out what he'd done, they'd be sure to send him to the police, and they put them in a box that makes them dead, and I couldn't bear to think of Bingo being dead. It came to me all of a sudden, how to put them off the scent, and I— I did it.

" I knew Betty and Hilary had had an awful quarrel just before," she continued. " So I messed up the study still worse, and I wrote that note and put it in the hearth. I know it was wicked, but after all I thought they wouldn't put Betty in a box and make her dead, but they'd do it to Bingo, and—and that's all, but I've been so unhappy ever since, and then I heard that Betty saved Bingo's life up on Beacon Hill. I couldn't keep it to myself any longer, and you can tell them it was me who did it if you like, but don't tell about Bingo, *please!*"

Never had Isabel made a speech of such length in the whole course of her young life, and never had the Terrible Twins listened to such a tragic confession. It almost took their breath away.

" Well, of all the *awful* things!" Madge said solemnly at last.

" I know it was awful," quavered Isabel. " I don't mind how I'm punished as long as Bingo doesn't get the blame."

To tell the truth, the twins were not thinking very much about Isabel and Bingo at that moment. They were remembering a certain evening, not so very long ago, when Miss Battle had called for three cheers for the heroine of the Cliff College match, and with remorse they remembered the shameful silence that had followed.

It was they who had started the campaign

against Betty, who had once been their idol. Believing she had played a mean trick on Hilary, they had persuaded the juniors to send her to Coventry, and only that morning there had been that scene in the hall, when they had hissed Betty instead of wishing her Many Happy Returns. And now it seemed that Betty had not been to blame at all, and that she had done nothing to deserve the snubs and slights they had put upon her.

" It's us who've been crazy and mean and wicked all the time," Maureen whispered. " Oh, it's like some awful nightmare! Why did we do those things against Betty, Madge? We used to know that Betty was one of the finest girls who ever breathed, and yet we— we——"

Never had the impulsive twins felt so troubled and angry with themselves.

" Are you going to tell Betty it was me?" questioned Isabel eagerly. " I don't care what you say, only please take care not to blame Bingo."

" Oh, don't worry about your precious puppy!" Madge cried. " We'll keep the secret, but it was terribly mean of you to write that note blaming it on Betty, Isabel. How could you have done it? Still, I suppose you were thinking of the dog, and—— But come along, Maureen. It's no good staying here. We've got to do something."

Hardly knowing what they meant to do, Madge and Maureen dashed out of the lumber-room, leaving Isabel still giving little sobs and wiping her eyes.

At the turn of the corridor, the twins almost bumped into Hilary, who eyed them somewhat coldly. Hilary had no wish to let the juniors think she approved of their action over the birthdays that morning, and she very well knew that Madge and Maureen were the ringleaders who had planned it all.

" Hilary!" they panted, in one breath.

" Well? What's the matter?"

" It's about Betty—about the way we've been treating her."

Hilary's grey eyes gazed at them candidly and coolly.

" If you ask my opinion about that, I think you were all very rude and unkind this morning," she replied. " Betty must have been terribly hurt, and as for me, it has quite spoilt my own birthday. Why did you do such a thing?"

" It was all a mistake, Hilary," exclaimed Madge. " I know we've treated Betty meanly, but we did it because we thought she ragged your study that time, and broke your statue."

Hilary was amazed.

" But what in the world made you think that ?" she asked.

" When we were helping you clear up the mess, we found a note with Betty's initials on it in the hearth," Maureen explained. " It said ' Serves you right '. It was just after you and Betty had quarrelled, Hilary—everybody knew about that—and, of course, we thought Betty had ragged your study to pay you out, and if she'd done something as rotten as that, she deserved to be sent to Coventry, didn't she? That's what we thought. But we didn't show you the note because we thought Betty might get into awful trouble about it—be expelled, or something like that."

" And this very minute we've discovered that it wasn't Betty at all," Madge took up the tale. " Someone left the note to lay the blame on Betty, but we'd rather not say who it was, and in a way it was an accident, Hilary. Nobody was to blame at all, in the first place."

" And now what are we to do ?" begged

Maureen. " How can we ever face Betty
again?"

Hilary gazed at their woebegone, troubled
faces.

" The best thing you can do is to go straight
to Betty and tell her what you have told me,"
she advised. " I'm sure she'll understand."

The twins looked at one another doubtfully.
Dare they face their one-time heroine with
such a dreadful confession to make?

" Yes, you're quite right, Hilary," Madge
said at last. " That's what we must do, though
I expect Betty will give us an awful scragging.
Come on, Maureen. Let's get it over."

Another rumble of thunder echoed through
the school as the twins scurried away, but
when they reached the door of Betty's study
they found it ajar, and the room empty. The
tea-bell rang before they had time to search
any further.

" Oh, golly!" sighed Madge. " There is
Miss Shephard's special meeting directly after
tea, so we shall have to wait till that's over.
I'm sure I shan't be able to eat a scrap."

However, though the twins were certainly
more silent than usual, it was noted that they
both made quite a good tea, and cleared up

the private pot of jam between them! Nothing short of an earthquake could have affected their healthy young appetites! From where they sat, they could not get a clear view of the senior tables, and so they did not see that Betty's place was vacant.

The seniors were glancing uncomfortably towards that vacant chair. It was Betty's birthday, and in the ordinary way she would have brought along some birthday cake and shared it with them all, and she would have been the centre of all the happy chatter over the tea-cups. But to-day her place was empty. Was it because she was upset by the ridiculous way in which the younger girls had behaved that morning? Or was it, more likely, that she had heard that Mary and Sonia had told Miss Shephard that afternoon that they were willing to act as prefects again, so that Betty herself was now the only remaining rebel? Or was she busy planning some protest at the meeting to be held after tea?

Hilary was the first to refer to the empty chair.

" Does anyone know where Betty is?" she asked.

Heads were shaken.

" Sonia and I went along to her study before tea, but she wasn't there," Mary said, looking even more solemn than usual. " We wanted to tell her we're going to be prefects again."

" Poor old Betty!" Esme Randall laughed lightly. " She takes things too much to heart, that's the trouble with her. Now, if only she was interested in something really important— like art or music—she would realize how petty all these schoolgirl squabbles are!"

Esme's tone was so utterly superior that everyone laughed.

" You ought to go on the stage, Esme darling," chuckled Hilda Field. " If you wore a monocle, and put on that comical drawl of yours, you would make any audience simply rock!"

Of course, it was fun to take Esme down a peg or two, but somehow the laughter and talk round the senior tables did not quite ring true. There was an air of expectancy about the girls; perhaps it was the effect of the strange storm which had been circling the district all the afternoon, but now seemed to be coming closer, as if before long it would burst in all its fury.

Not a drop of rain had fallen yet, but gusts

of wind rattled doors and windows, and now and again the dark sky was lit up by a stab of lightning. For many weeks now the weather had been unusually fine and dry, but to-night it seemed that the spell would be broken.

There was little talking as the girls hurried from the dining-room into the hall, where Miss Shephard was going to talk to them. As soon as they were in their places the head mistress entered and made her way to the desk on the platform.

Hilary, glancing anxiously around, saw that Betty was the only girl not present. As they had entered the hall, the twins had managed to inform her of their failure to find Betty and make their confession. Would Betty have been here now if she had learnt the truth? Would it have made things easier for her if she had known that the juniors' actions had all been due to a mistake? Or was it just her queer loyalty to her old head mistress that made her stay away from Miss Shephard's meeting?

A puzzled look came to Hilary's grey eyes.

" It's rather strange," she thought. " Betty and I always have been enemies, but I'm worried about her just as—just as if she were my friend."

Miss Shephard was speaking now. What a handsome figure she made as she stood at the desk, the light falling on her coils of jet-black hair! Her fine dark eyes rested on the assembled girls, and her ringing contralto voice clearly reached every corner of the hall. There was something very magnetic about the new head, and even the smallest girl was held to rapt attention.

Miss Shephard spoke first of the storm that was gathering overhead.

" Scientists tell us that storms are Nature's way of restoring a proper balance in the air," she said. " When the pressure in one part of the atmosphere is too great, and in another part too small, then a storm breaks to put things right. A storm doesn't upset things, really, girls—it is just Nature putting her house in order.

" This Windmill School, which we all love so much, has had its own storms and its times of stress, but they, too, may have been just as needful as the storms that put our atmosphere to rights. Perhaps some of you may feel that we are having rather a stormy term, but I feel sure we shall all be the better for the difficulties we have had to face."

For a moment Miss Shephard paused, her eyes glancing over the rows of fresh girlish faces turned up to her. Her gaze rested for a brief second on the empty seat which Betty Lyndon should have occupied, and then she went on:

" At the beginning of this term our prefects felt they could no longer go on acting because they felt that I—as your new head mistress— was making changes that would injure the spirit of the school. Though I was grieved, yet I did try to understand them, and I knew they were acting from a sense of loyalty to Windmill. That was why I did not replace them, and I am glad to tell you that they have all—except one—agreed to take up their prefectships again.

" Don't think I am unmindful of the traditions of the school, my dear girls. Your late head mistress, Miss Jennings, is a very dear friend of mine, and she herself knew that changes were necessary, though she felt too old to carry them through herself.

" Don't be afraid of change, girls! Try to realize that the present and the future may be more important than the past. In Windmill I want us to achieve a forward-looking spirit.

To take one matter that I know has troubled some of you, my decision to convert the old windmill common-room into a modern laboratory.

" Think, my dears! A girl trained in our new laboratory may one day become a famous woman doctor or scientist who may make discoveries of vast importance to her fellow human beings. Is not that more important than merely preserving a relic of the past? Don't you realize that those who would stop such a change are perhaps blocking the path of progress? Don't let it be said that, at Windmill, we prefer the past to the present or the future!"

For some minutes the head spoke in this strain. Her deep sincerity, and the kindling accents of her voice, made the girls forget the storm that was thundering outside. Hardly a movement was made in those listening ranks till Miss Shephard concluded her little speech. Then the girls, by one accord, broke into loud and prolonged clapping.

It was a great tribute to Miss Shephard's character and personality, and Hilary felt very proud of her brilliant aunt at that moment. But at the back of Hilary's mind a question kept asking itself: Where was Betty? What was Betty doing and thinking now?

Miss Shephard was smiling, for she was aware that she had won the girls over to her side.

" I would like the prefects publicly to say that they are willing to serve again," she went on. " Then I wish to make a little presentation. I will ask you one by one, girls. Do you wish to serve again, Hilda Field?"

" Yes, Miss Shephard."

" And you, Esme Randall?"

" Yes, Miss Shephard."

" And you, Sonia Starforth?"

" Oh yes, Miss Shephard, I——"

" And you, Mary Towle?"

" Yes, Miss Shephard."

There was a slight pause. Everyone was thinking of one name that had not been mentioned.

" Will you four girls please step forward, together with Hilary," went on the head.

The five of them stepped out in front, and to their surprise and delight, Miss Shephard presented each with a little silver brooch, in the shape of a windmill.

" That is our new prefect's badge," smiled the head. "And now I will ask the girls to give their prefects a good clap."

Once again there was an outburst of clapping, and while it was going on, Miss Shephard walked to the door, leaving the girls thronging round the prefects, demanding a closer look at their new badges of office.

To her surprise, Miss Shephard found Andrew McTavish, the gardener, waiting outside the door, resting on a stick. The previous evening Andrew had slipped in his back yard and twisted his ankle badly, and was now forced to hobble.

" What is it, Andrew?"

" Begging your pardon, ma'am, but I thocht ye ought to know about yon wee lassie who's crying her heart out in the old windmill room yonder. I heard the sound o' it as I passed by, and I peeped in, but she didna see me. Ye'll forgive me, ma'am, but I'm thinking Miss Betty is in sore distress."

Andrew hobbled a pace closer.

" She's a guid lassie, ma'am. I've known her for years, long before her mither died—and she's a guid wee bairn."

Miss Shephard gave Andrew her brilliant, kindly smile.

" I am glad you told me, Andrew," she replied. " I am sorry to think any of my girls should be so unhappy here. I will go to Betty at once."

Bareheaded, Miss Shephard crossed the courtyard, and as she did so, there was a vivid flash of lightning and a deafening thunder-clap. Not for one moment did the head mis-tress falter, and she reached the door of the old senior common-room.

The lockers and most of the other furniture had already been taken away, but the lighting had not been interfered with yet. The room was in darkness, and Miss Shephard stretched out her hand and switched on the light.

On the opposite wall hung the portrait of Miss Priscilla Jennings, which had not been taken down, and on the floor beneath it knelt a crumpled, brown-haired figure, her head resting against the wall, her body now and again shaken by sobs.

There was such a look of despair and lone-liness in Betty's posture that Miss Shephard's heart was touched. Till now she had been apt to regard Betty as a troublesome girl, and the ringleader of those who had rebelled against her authority. Now, as she gazed at that for-lorn figure, she asked herself if she had ever done justice to the strength of Betty's feelings, if she had ever tried to understand that strange, passionate loyalty to the old head of Windmill School.

Miss Shephard took a step or two forward.

" Betty, my dear," she said gently.

Her voice was like a signal that brought Betty to life, and the girl leapt to her feet, tossing back her thick brown hair, and looking at Miss Shephard with haggard, troubled eyes.

Before the head mistress could speak again, she burst out:

" I can't stay here! I don't belong to Windmill any more! It's all strange, and hateful!"

Before Miss Shephard could stop her, she had darted past, and rushed out into the darkness and the storm.

" Betty! Come back! Come back!"

The head's ringing call was drowned by a burst of thunder, and when Miss Shephard reached the door, there was no sign of the rebel schoolgirl, and though she hurried towards the gate, calling again and again, no answer came.

Five minutes later the news was all over the school. Betty Lyndon had run away!

CHAPTER XIV

The Search in the Storm

Windmill School stood in a lonely stretch of country, bordered on the south by Beacon Hill and many miles of moorland, while to the north wound the country road leading to the village of Old Cross. If Betty seriously meant to run away, it was thought most likely that she had taken this road and was making for Old Cross railway station, six miles from the school.

It was now half-past six. Hasty reference to a time-table showed that there was a London train leaving Old Cross at eight-thirty.

" Betty has an aunt in London," Miss Shephard said, closing the time-table and looking up at Miss Darkin. " That is her only relative in England, I believe. It seems almost certain, does it not, that Betty would think first of going to her aunt?"

Miss Darkin nodded, and then looked doubtful.

" If she ran off without hat or coat, would

she have the money to pay for her fare?" she
wondered.

" I think it quite likely she had some money
with her," Miss Shephard said. " If not, she
might try to board the train and rely on her
aunt paying at the other end. Yes, I feel sure
the railway station is the first place to try."

The window-curtains of the head's study had
not been drawn, and at that moment a vivid
flash of lightning lit the darkness outside,
followed by a tremendous roll of thunder.
Miss Darkin shivered a little.

" Poor child!" she exclaimed. " What a
night to be out in the open, alone and unhappy!"

Miss Shephard was already at the telephone,
putting through a call to the stationmaster at
Old Cross, warning him to keep a look-out for
a wandering schoolgirl.

" I think you and I will get the car out and
go to Old Cross ourselves, Miss Darkin," decided the head. " We will drive slowly, and
possibly we may catch sight of Betty on the
road. I do not want to alarm her aunt until we
have exhausted all means of finding her."

In ten minutes the car was starting away,
with Miss Shephard herself at the wheel, while

several other mistresses set off to search in different directions.

Hilary, standing at the door looking into the courtyard, sighed anxiously.

" If there only had been time for Madge and Maureen to tell Betty all about the ragged study, and explain what an awful mistake it was!" she thought. " That might have made all the difference. Oh, I'm beginning to understand how jolly unhappy Betty must have been!"

After her usual fashion, Hilary was blaming herself. She felt she had not done her duty, that she ought to have taken steps to make friends with Betty, instead of allowing their enmity to grow; that above all she ought to have checked the juniors in their cruel thoughtless nonsense about sending Betty to Coventry.

" I knew it was going on," Hilary admitted to herself. " At least, I heard rumours that it was, and I—I suppose I was glad to think I was first favourite with the youngsters instead of Betty!"

A halting step sounded behind her, and looking round she saw Andrew McTavish, leaning on his stick.

" Och! 'Tis maself that's angry with maself

to-nicht," exclaimed the old man. " Wi' this crocked foot, I canna help search for the lassie."

" Auntie's doing everything possible, Andrew," replied Hilary. " She has just driven away to the station with Miss Darkin, and other mistresses are out on the search too. Don't worry. They'll find her!"

Andrew coughed.

" There's a fancy in my head that I canna get rid of," he said. " I wouldna tell the head mistress, for fear she'd think 'twas just an old man's foolishness, and maybe 'tis just that. But yet——"

" Why, Andrew, what is it?" cried Hilary, her hand on the old gardener's sleeve. " Do you mean you have some idea where Betty might have gone to?"

" Ye might call it that, I reckon," said Andrew. " Ye see, the bairn was mighty fond o' Miss Jennings, the old head mistress; I'm thinking she gave her some o' the love she'd ha' given to her ain mother, if she'd had one. Be that as it may, I met the lassie on Beacon Hill not so long ago, and she told me she climbed the Beacon Tower just for a sight o' the wee house, away to the south, where Miss

Jennings went to live—aye, and she said she'd dearly like to gae up there one nicht, to see the light twinkling in the window. A strange fancy, ye'll think, and yet 'tis in my mind that the lassie may ha' gone up there."

" You mean, you think Betty may be climbing Beacon Hill in this storm?" gasped Hilary.

The old man nodded.

" I doot it'll be just foolishness on my part," he said. " But that's what's stuck in my mind, and if it wasna for this pesky ankle, that's the way I'd look for Miss Betty."

Muttering to himself, Andrew hobbled away, leaving Hilary's thoughts in a turmoil.

Could it be possible that Andrew was right? In her hour of trouble and despair, had Betty fled away, careless of the storm, to the tower from which she could see her old friend's windows twinkling through the gloom? Beacon Tower! People said that the tower was not safe, and that it was dangerous to climb those worn stone steps. What would it be like on such a night as this, with the thunder and the wind and the lightning all around it?

Hilary had her full share of schoolgirl pluck, but she was frightened of storms, though she would not often confess it. Especially the roll-

ing of thunder aroused in her a strange unreasoning fear.

Yet now her grey eyes saw the path of duty
clearly before her. It was her duty to search
for Betty on Beacon Hill, and to tell her about
the ragged study and the misunderstandings
that had followed it. To tell her that Madge
and Maureen and the others were truly sorry,
and that there would be nothing but warm
and happy welcome for her, if she would turn
back to school.

" I couldn't explain all that to Auntie or the
mistresses," thought Hilary. " Besides, they're
not here. I've got to do it myself, on my
own!"

She had an electric torch in her locker, and
she fetched it, and then hurried to the cloak-
room and slipped on her mackintosh. A few
moments later she was letting herself out of the
school gate and taking the lane that curved
round to the moor.

Still there was no rain, and the rustling of
the wind in dry bushes and trees sounded
weirdly. Passing the hockey field, Hilary found
herself facing the open moorland, with the dark
bulk of Beacon Hill rising from it, and as she
gazed, a sliver of lightning struck downwards

at the very hill itself, or so it seemed. Hilary put her fingers over her ears to shut out the crash of thunder that she knew would follow.

The beam of her torch making a white pool of light on the ground in front of her, Hilary hastened on, bending low as the wind buffeted her. At the foot of the hill she was caught unawares by another echoing thunder - clap which awoke all her unreasoning terrors.

" I can't—I can't go on!" she whispered, half turning. " I can't face it!"

As she turned, the torch ray swung round too, and suddenly lit up something white lying against a bush. It was a handkerchief, and stifling her fears, Hilary stooped and picked it up, looking at it closely. In one corner were embroidered the initials " B. L.".

So it was true, then! Betty had passed this way on her flight from the school, and, as Andrew had guessed, she must have been making for the Beacon Tower, unless indeed she meant to press on all the way to Miss Jennings's house.

The handkerchief lay there in Hilary's hand, and somehow the sight and feel of it were enough to bring back her courage. A moment

before she had whispered: " I can't go on!"
Now she thought: " I can't turn back!"

Her face almost as pale as the handkerchief,
her lips set tightly, Hilary began the climb.
The path wound between masses of dry bushes,
all of which gave out that strange dry rustling
sound.   Hilary forced herself to ignore the
lightning and the thunder. She kept her eyes
fixed on the pool of light made by her torch,
and steadily she climbed higher.

Once she paused, trembling in every limb,
and glanced upwards.   At first all was dark,
but then a fresh flicker of lightning showed her
the outlines of the tower, vividly etched for
one fleeting second. Was it her fancy, or did
she see the head and shoulders of a figure
behind the parapet of the tower-top?

" Betty!   Betty!" Hilary shouted, knowing
her voice must be drowned by wind and
thunder long before it could reach that lonely
figure, if indeed there was someone there.

Though she had felt her limbs would not
support her another yard, Hilary found strength
to plod upwards again.   It seemed to her that
the storm was fiercer here, as though the top
of Beacon Hill were the very heart of it.

" Oh, God, take care of Betty—take care

of me too!" she breathed through dry lips.

The bushes pressed thickly about her. The fear came to her that she might have missed the path, and be nearing the dreadful precipice of Highwayman's Cliff. Her heart sank as she saw that the torch was burning lower—she had forgotten that the battery was almost used up—and recklessly she struggled forward, knowing that soon she must be in pitch darkness, except for such fitful gleams as the lightning gave.

The torch flickered suddenly, and went out.

With a cry, Hilary dropped it, careless where it fell. Her arms outstretched, she groped forward, and then a quavering gasp of thankfulness came from her, for her fingers had touched crumbling stonework, and she knew she had reached Beacon Tower at last.

Frantically she felt her way along till she reached the narrow open doorway which admitted to a small paved porch from which the winding stair rose up. A rumble of thunder seemed to shake the tower, and feeling that she was almost at the end of her tether, Hilary found the foot of the stairway and began to climb up.

" Betty! Betty!" she called hoarsely.

She had reached the fifth or sixth step when there was a splitting, cracking sound, and Hilary's feet slid away beneath her in the midst of a great crashing. The stone stairway in Beacon Tower had long been known to be unsafe; now at last it had given way beneath Hilary's weight, the lower steps collapsing without warning, Hilary in their midst.

She had not climbed very high, luckily, but she fell heavily, and at once became aware of a darting pain in her ankle. Something was pressing on it; one of the stones had fallen in such a way that her ankle was twisted and trapped, and try as she would, she could not free herself. The horror of it brought a cry of "Help! Oh, help!" from her lips.

There was a brief lull in the storm, and in the strange hush Hilary could hear movements above, and they brought both relief and alarm to her.

" Take care!" she called, her voice sounding strangely cracked and thin. " The stairs have broken at the bottom. I'm caught down here, under the stone. Oh, Betty, is it you?"

A pause, during which she heard more cautious movements. Then unmistakably she heard Betty's voice:

" Yes, it's me. Who is it down there?"

" Hilary!"

There was no answer to this. It seemed that Betty was cautiously feeling her way downwards, and Hilary's heart was in her mouth for fear she should hear again the crash and fall of stone. But Betty had safely reached the gap where the steps had given way, about five feet from the bottom.

" Where are you?" she called. " I'm going to lower myself down, and I don't want to drop on you."

" I've fallen here—nearer the door!" Hilary replied, rather faintly.

Betty was kneeling, gripping the edge of the broken stonework and lowering herself, till she stood amidst the broken fragments of stone in the porch. Moving carefully, she touched Hilary's leg, and then found the stone that was trapping it. She gripped it firmly and tugged upwards, moving it only a fraction of an inch, but enough for Hilary to drag her foot free with a little gasp of pain.

It was pitch dark, and neither girl could see the other, but it seemed to Hilary that Betty was kneeling down beside her.

" Are you hurt—except your ankle, I mean?"

" No, I don't think so. It's sprained, I'm afraid—or badly twisted."

" Better not take the shoe off. Better keep it on—it checks the swelling."

Still the lull in the storm persisted, but the girls were talking in whispers, almost as if they feared to raise their voices. In the darkness, Betty tossed the brown hair back from her forehead.

" How did you know I was here? Why did you come?" she asked, very low.

" Auntie—Miss Shephard—thought you had gone to the station, but Andrew said he had a strange feeling you might be up here. He couldn't search himself, because of his hurt foot, and—oh, Betty, I so much wanted to find you. If you've been bothered about the way the juniors have behaved, I want to tell you it's all due to a mistake. Madge and Maureen told me so to-day; they found it out this very day, and they've been trying to find you and tell you how sorry they were. They're awfully cut up. You see, my study was ragged some time ago, and one or two things I value very much were broken. The twins thought you had done it; they found something they thought was proof, and you know how impulsive they are.

That was why they started that stupid Coventry business, and now they know for certain it wasn't you at all, and—and——"

Hilary's flow of words came to an end.

" I'm so glad I've found you," she whispered, catching her voice on a sob. " Not only for that, but—but you're braver than I am, Betty, and I've been so scared of the storm."

Betty's hand reached out and found Hilary's, and pressed it gently, and in that moment whatever enmity there had been between the two girls vanished for always.

There was no time for further explanations. Betty was given no chance to explain just why she had climbed Beacon Hill in the storm, and Hilary was given no opportunity to persuade her to return.

That pause in the storm had been only deceptive. Like a cunning fighter, the tempest had pretended to withdraw, so that it might launch a final blow with shattering effect.

The porch and the tower and the bush-covered hillside were suddenly lit up with a vivid glare, such as the girls had never seen before, and this was accompanied by a terrifying peal of thunder that made Hilary cling trembling to Betty. In the midst of all this another sound could be heard, a dull crash, and then half-way down the hill a red glow of flame shone out.

" Something's been struck by lightning," cried Betty, peering through the door. " A tree, it must be—and it's caught fire. There's a regular bonfire down there amongst the bushes."

The wind moaned weirdly, fanning the flames, and Betty sprang to her feet.

" It's a regular bush fire!" she exclaimed. " Everything is so dry, it will burn like tinder, and there hasn't been a drop of rain so far. Hilary! The wind's blowing it up this way; it is spreading every moment."

The glow of the fire already made a faint ghostly light inside the porch. Betty turned, bending over Hilary.

" It wouldn't be safe to stay here, anyway,' she said quickly. " Now that the stairway has collapsed, there's no telling when the whole tower may come tumbling on top of us. And if that fire spreads up here, we'll be caught in the middle of it."

" But I—I can't walk," Hilary said faintly. Then she added, in a stronger tone: " I'm not going to hang on to you, and stop you. I'll be quite all right in here while you go down the other side of the hill and fetch help."

Betty's answer was to stoop lower and grasp Hilary under the arm-pits.

" I don't want to hurt you, old thing," she said lightly. " Try to stand on one leg. I'm going to carry you, part of the way at any rate. And please don't raise objections, because I'm just a wee bit deaf in the ear nearest to you!"

What a gay, confident note there was in Betty's voice now! It was a note that had rarely been heard during the past troubled weeks at school, but in facing this danger from storm and fire, Betty had found herself again, and for the time being her cares were forgotten. It was not for nothing that she came of a long line of soldiers who, in many perilous places, had served their country well.

Hilary had plenty of courage too, but it was of rather a different kind, and in the midst of actual physical danger she needed someone to cling to and rely on. Grimacing a little with pain, she rose obediently, and with an effort Betty lifted her and stepped through the narrow doorway.

Both girls were startled by the way in which

the bush fire had already been fanned into a crimson furnace. The wind lashed the flames, driving them on, and plainly to be heard was the hiss and crackle of burning wood and leaf. Within living memory, so it was said afterwards, there had never been such a fire so late in October, or such a storm either.

The fire had spread so far to either side, as well as advancing upwards, that to the minds of both girls came the fear that it might encircle the hill, trapping them before they could reach a safety zone.

" It's a good thing you're on the thin side, Hilary!" panted Betty, with a little laugh. " You're no weight at all."

Her arm round Betty's neck, Hilary said nothing. They turned the corner of the tower, and slowly began the descent on the other side, but still all around them was the strange lurid glow, and thunder still rumbled overhead.

At least there was no difficulty in seeing the path, and for some minutes Betty struggled on steadily with her burden, till aching arms and want of breath forced her to set Hilary gently down.

" Just for two secs!" she panted.

Hilary caught her hand.

" Betty! I can smell fire, and—and see it, all around. I believe we're trapped!"

With a queer shining look in her eyes, Betty was gazing down the hill.

" We're not trapped," she said. " Can't you see that light twinkling away down there, like a star, Hilary? That's the light in Prissy's house—our dear old head, you know—and that's the way we're going!"

As if the vision of the twinkling light had given her new strength, Betty stooped and picked Hilary up again, and once more struggled on. Her eyes were fixed on the distant light, and she had no breath to spare for words. Hilary clung limply, trying to ignore the stabbing pain in her ankle, and now and again glancing at Betty's rapt and steadfast face. It seemed to Hilary that she had never known Betty truly till now; never known how strong and loyal she was.

Hilary felt dreadfully hot. It must be that the fire was closer to them; at any moment, turning a corner of the path, they might see that the flames had raced ahead of them and were barring their way. Hilary closed her eyes as she thought of that dreadful fate, to be trapped in the midst of the blazing heath.

No longer did Betty seem to require rest or breathing space. Her breath was coming quickly, and Hilary fancied she could feel her beating heart, but not once did she falter.

" Betty! Put me down, and rest!"

The only answer was a panting laugh, and Betty's eyes never left the starry light that was guiding her. On and on, down that seemingly endless hill.

Then to their ears came a fresh sound—a pattering, hissing, sighing sound, all around them, and on their faces and their hands. And now at last Betty found her voice.

" Rain!" she croaked hoarsely. " It's come at last! Never mind if we get drenched; there's no more danger from the fire, for the rain will put it out. Listen to it, Hilary! Isn't it the grandest thing you ever heard?"

As Betty said, it was a grateful sound. It was lovely to think of those hungry leaping flames being smothered by this downpour from the dark heavens, that had been so long delayed. They raised their faces to it, like thirsty creatures in a parched land.

Then Betty caught sight of two glowing lights moving not far in front.

" We've nearly reached the lane at the bottom

of the hill, and there's a car going along it. Come on, Hil! Shout—shout for all you're worth, and they may hear us!"

A pair of young voices shouted through the rainy darkness:

" Help! Help!"

CHAPTER XV

Friends Meet Again

The storm was over. In the house called Travellers' Rest, the sound of gently falling rain penetrated a quiet room lit by a carefully shaded lamp. A fire glowed in the hearth, and beside it sat a white-haired lady with a heavy bandage around her eyes.

She sat with folded hands, and yet there was something alert about her attitude, as if she was listening, expecting, waiting for something or someone.

It was Miss Priscilla Jennings, and that bandage around her eyes spoke of many things— of days and weeks of suffering and darkness, of periods when the sickness of the eyes troubled the brain, and even memory went and there was nothing in the world but pain and the horror of blindness. The hands of a skilled surgeon had been at work, but not until that bandage was removed would it be known whether the kindly eyes would ever see again.

The clock on the mantelpiece ticked steadily, against the window-pane the rain pattered and sighed, and the cat on the hearthrug stretched himself and lazily blinked his green and glowing eyes.

The door opened suddenly. In her anxiety for her mistress, Miss Jennings's trim maid had forgotten to knock.

"I can hear a car, miss. It's turning in the drive!"

"Yes, Mary, I hear it too. I have no doubt it is Sir Harold."

Miss Jennings's voice was unexpectedly calm and steady, as if whatever ordeal she had been through had not lessened the quiet courage of her spirit.

"Oh, miss, I hope everything is going to be all right, I do indeed."

"Thank you, Mary. It helps me to think I have kind friends such as you."

The door-bell rang, and with a gulp and something like a sob, Mary withdrew. The famous surgeon who had performed the operation on Miss Jennings's eyes was already at the door, and to-night he would remove the bandage that had been worn ever since, and that white-haired figure by the fire would know whether she would ever use her eyes again.

Voices, footsteps, could be heard in the hall, and Miss Jennings recognized Sir Harold's deep confident tones.

The cat on the hearthrug mewed uneasily, and then suddenly sprang on Miss Jennings's lap.

"What is the matter, Samson? What is troubling you?"

Feeling those well-known fingers tickling his cheek and stroking his sleek fur, Samson settled down and began to purr loudly. The voices and footsteps could no longer be heard; no doubt Mary had shown the distinguished visitor into another room.

The purring of the cat, the ticking of the clock, the sighing of rain against the windowpane; things heard, but not seen.

Then the sound of quick footsteps, and the opening door, and Mary's voice announcing Sir Harold. Miss Jennings smiled and held out her hand, and the surgeon gripped it firmly, confidently, hopefully, as it seemed. When the first greetings were over, Miss Jennings said:

"I feel sure I heard girls' voices when you

entered the hall, Sir Harold. Yet it seems so strange that they should be here that I am wondering if it was my fancy. But no! I am sure I heard Betty Lyndon's voice."

The surgeon laughed softly.

"You heard them, sure enough. My chauffeur and I found two girls on the hillside out there, and they seemed to have escaped from all the dangers imaginable—storm, fire, and I don't know what—with no more harm than a twisted ankle. To my amazement, I found that one of them was my niece Hilary. I brought them along here, and your maid is fitting them up with dry clothes."

" Does Betty—know?"

" Yes, she knows, for I told her myself. I gathered she was a very dear and particular friend of yours. It is not she who has sprained her ankle, it is Hilary. Betty is—well, she's thinking of you."

Miss Jennings drew a deep breath.

" I was their head mistress, as you know, Sir Harold, and Betty is one of my dearest friends. I didn't want to burden their young hearts with my troubles. I told Miss Shephard not to let any of them know—even Betty— till the operation was decided one way or the

other. They had a new head, and a new term,
and I wanted them to face it all without any
worry about me; perhaps I might have changed
my mind where Betty is concerned, but you
know how ill I have been. I couldn't reflect,
couldn't remember. And now, Betty is here."

Miss Jennings's hand groped up till it found
the surgeon's arm.

" Sir Harold! I feel I would like Betty to be
in the room when you take this bandage off.
Would it be asking too much of her, do you
think?"

" My dear lady, if I am any judge of character, Betty is a girl who would do anything
in the world to help you. Yes, she shall surely
be here. I will fetch her myself."

Again that bandaged figure in the chair
waited, listening, her fingers smoothing Samson's fur. Now the footsteps were returning,
but this time there was another step—a light,
quick step. Betty had entered the room, and
she had darted noiselessly across and seized
those thin white hands.

" I'm here, dear Miss Jennings, and I'm so
glad to be here too. I never knew—never
dreamt——"

" No, my dear, you couldn't have dreamt.

But I feel it is the finger of Providence that has brought you here to-night. Sit down opposite to me, Betty—and wait."

Sir Harold was adjusting the special lamp, turning it down slightly, making sure that it would not be too strong for those eyes if, by good fortune, vision had returned. He quietly placed a screen before the fire.

Betty's gaze never left her white-haired friend. Her face was pale, her lips trembling, but her eyes were dry, for she felt somehow beyond tears; her whole being was concentrated in one heart-shaking prayer that those kind eyes might see.

Gently the surgeon was removing the bandage, fold by fold, talking in his steady confident way. None knew better than he that the result of the operation was extremely doubtful; it might well be that his patient was permanently blind. No hint of his uncertainty, however, could be guessed from his tone of voice.

" Don't be surprised at what may happen when the last fold is off," he was saying. " You may see nothing at first, or you may get a blurred vision which should quickly sharpen. The light in here is very soft, nothing to hurt your eyes at all. There, now. It's off!"

Miss Jennings was looking straight towards Betty, and for one hushed moment she said nothing. Then she smiled.

" Betty, my dear! I see you—you're becoming clearer every moment!"

They were simple words, spoken in a quiet tone, but in them was all the difference between darkness and light. With a little cry that was half a sob, Betty threw herself on to the rug at her old friend's feet, clasping her hands.

" Oh, I'm so happy!"

Stroking the wavy brown hair of the rebel schoolgirl, Miss Jennings looked up at the surgeon who had saved her sight. Though she was so familiar with his voice and touch, it was the first time she had actually seen him.

" You have given me back my eyes, Sir Harold," she said gently. " I can't say—I needn't tell you—how deeply grateful I feel at this moment." Miss Jennings smiled. " You will forgive me, but what a striking likeness there is between you and your sister! Betty, I think I should introduce you properly to Sir Harold Shephard, your head mistress's brother."

Betty looked up with an odd light in her eyes. Hilary had already told her just who

Sir Harold was, and she had seen for herself the likeness between the surgeon and Miss Shephard.

" I—I'm grateful to you too, Sir Harold!" she burst out. " I never dreamed Miss Shephard had a brother who was a surgeon. I—I thought her brother was a famous artist. At least, Esme said that—that——"

She broke off in confusion, and Sir Harold laughed.

" Your head mistress has two brothers, as it happens, young lady," he explained. " My brother John is an artist, and I am a surgeon. And speaking as your head mistress's brother," he went on, with a twinkle in his eye, " I think we should ring up the school and tell them that the two wanderers have been found. I will do so myself. May I use your telephone in the other room, Miss Jennings?"

" Please do, Sir Harold," replied Betty's old friend. " And if Miss Shephard does not object, will you tell her that I should like to keep the girls here for to-night. I guarantee to send them both back safely in the morning."

The surgeon left the room, and Miss Jennings pointed to a fireside chair close to her.

" Sit there, Betty. You and I have such a

lot to say to each other. And you must introduce me to your friend, Hilary. How strange you should have been rescued by Hilary's uncle! I am so glad that you and she are friends."

" Yes, we're friends," said Betty. " From to-night."

Those understanding eyes looked at Betty, and perhaps they noted the signs of strain and unhappiness that could be seen there.

" I so much want to hear all about everything, Betty. You see, I've been too ill to write to you, my dear, and I had made up my mind not to worry you with my troubles during those few weeks of your new term with Miss Shephard. But now I'm hungry for news!"

Betty glanced at the door.

" Do you think Sir Harold would mind? Perhaps he thinks you are not strong enough to talk yet."

" But I don't want to talk," smiled Miss Jennings. " I want you to talk, Betty, here and now. Tell me everything, my dear!"

It was what Betty needed, more than anything else, to release those pent-up feelings which she had kept in her heart for too long. She poured out the story of her rebellion, and the misunderstandings that had added to her troubles, knowing that in her beloved old friend she would find the most understanding listener of all.

Sir Harold was a long time making his connexion, and after that he went to see how Hilary was getting on, so Betty had plenty of time. What a relief it was to tell the whole story!

"Do you think I've been—foolish?" she asked, in the end.

"No, my dear, you've been trying to be loyal, and loyalty is one of the finest things in the world. I'm sure I don't know what we can put above it. You know, Betty, I'm beginning to blame myself, just a little."

"Blame yourself?" cried Betty. "After all you've been through—all the pain and the illness and everything?"

"Yes, but I see now that I should have told you about it all, in the first place, my dear. I think things were much harder for you, just because you didn't hear from me. It made you all the more determined to be loyal, as you thought."

Betty pressed her friend's hand.

"Yes, perhaps it did," she whispered.

"And then there were those misunderstandings which have been cleared away now," went on Miss Jennings. "Really, I think the storm is over, Betty. And I want you to understand that Miss Shephard is a very wonderful woman. It was she who interested her brother in my case. He is one of the most famous eye surgeons in the world, and I could never have afforded his skill and care, if it had not been for Miss Shephard's great kindness. She comes of a brilliant family, and Windmill School is lucky to have such a brilliant head mistress.

"And I ought to make a little confession to you too," smiled Miss Jennings. "I knew that Windmill needed change, just as everything needs it, though I felt too old to carry through those changes myself. I feel happy about the school because I know it is in such good hands, my dear."

Something of the old, merry, care-free look had come back to Betty's face.

"I'm beginning to feel happy about Windmill—and everything else too," she whispered.

CHAPTER XVI

All's Well with Windmill!

It was a week later.

Feet pattered on worn paving stones, dark heads and fair heads bobbed excitedly as the girls of Windmill School, seniors and juniors, made their way across the courtyard. There was a buzz of voices, happy and excited.

" Betty and Hilary have called a special meeting!"

" I'm sure I don't know how we're all going to cram into the Windmill common-room! Isn't it strange that Miss Shephard has had all the furniture put back! I thought it was going to be turned into a lab!"

" Hilary and Betty are in with Miss Shephard now."

" What I want to know," asked Mary Towle solemnly, " is whether Betty saved Hilary's life on Beacon Hill, or whether Hilary saved Betty's. You see, I'm writing a poem about it, and I want to make sure."

" Better say that they saved each other's

lives," laughed Esme. "Then you can't be wrong, Miss Shakespeare!"

Esme was feeling very happy these days. John Shephard had seen her drawings, and been struck by them; he had promised to help her get the training she needed so much, and it looked as if her dreams were going to have a chance to come true!

"I'm so thrilled about Hilary and Betty making up their feud," exclaimed Sonia. "Because it reminds me of one of my ancestors who fought in the Crusades. He saved the life of his enemy, a noble Saracen, and always after that they were firm friends, though, of course, they still had to go on fighting each other, because they were on different sides, and——"

Sonia broke off, as something scampered between her feet. It was a shaggy puppy, Bingo by name, and Isabel Bayley was hot in pursuit of him.

Somehow Miss Shephard had found out that Bingo had played a part in the events of the term, and possibly she had heard the story of how Isabel had rescued him and cared for him by stealth. At any rate, an exception had been made in the rule that no dogs were allowed, and Bingo had been installed as the school mascot, with Isabel Bayley as his guardian, much to that queer child's joy.

Into the old windmill common-room they crowded, laughing and chattering and filling almost every inch of space.

" Here come Hilary and Betty, arm in arm," exclaimed Madge, who with her twin had got a post of vantage on one of the window-sills. " Let's give them both a jolly good cheer!"

Henceforth the twins were going to have two idols—Betty and Hilary—and give to each an equal meed of worship. Their lusty young voices rose above the general cheers as Hilary and Betty entered the common-room. Hilary still limped a little, but otherwise was none the worse for her night adventure on Beacon Hill.

As for Betty, she was looking radiantly happy. She was a prefect once again, and thanks to the happenings on that night of storm and fire, her troubles had rolled away.

" Take the big chair, Betty!" smiled Esme.

" No, that's for Hilary, because she's got a crocked foot," Betty said. " I'm going to take the table!"

Just as she had done at that earlier meeting at the beginning of term, Betty vaulted on the table, gazing around with shining eyes, and tossing the wavy brown hair away from her forehead.

" I've only got two things to tell you, girls!" she cried. " We've just been seeing Miss Shephard, and what do you think she told us? She feels that some of us are very fond of this old windmill common-room, and that perhaps it was a mistake to want to change it. That is what the head told me to tell you, girls, and we're going to keep our old senior common-room, and the new lab will be built somewhere else. We're all ever so grateful to Miss Shephard, and I'm going to ask you to give her three jolly good cheers!"

It is surprising what a loud cheer a crowd of schoolgirls can raise. Bingo, the puppy, was so alarmed that his guardian thought it prudent to put her fingers over his ears till the noise had subsided!

" And there's something else," went on Betty. " Perhaps you all know by now that our late head—dear Miss Priscilla Jennings—has been very ill, and if it had not been for the wonderful skill of Miss Shephard's brother—not the artist, Esme, the surgeon—she would have lost her sight. Miss Jennings is as well as ever now, and she is coming to visit the school this very afternoon, and stay to tea, and——"

Betty paused. From her post on the table, she could see through the window towards the main school gateway, and she had just caught sight of Miss Jennings's car turning in.

A moment later, the tall figure of Miss Shephard could be seen hurrying forward to greet her visitor.

" Here she is!" cried Betty. " Miss Shephard is shaking hands with her, and—and I do believe they are coming straight here. Yes, they are. Take a deep breath, girls, and pull yourselves together, and let's give the loudest cheer ever heard in this or any other school. Are you ready? Than let it go!"

The new head and the white-haired, smiling visitor were greeted by a storm of cheering that threatened to lift the roof, and that was surely proof that once more all was well with Windmill School.

" It's all right, Bingo darling," whispered Isabel Bayley, trying to close the puppy's ears and hug him at the same time. " There's nothing to be scared of. They're just cheering because they're happy!"